LUNE IT

Dan Grujic

MINERVA PRESS

LONDON

ATLANTA MONTREUX SYDNEY

LUNE IT
Copyright © Dan Grujic 1998

ISBN 0 75410 299 8

First Published 1998 by
MINERVA PRESS
195 Knightsbridge
London SW7 1RE

Printed in Great Britain for Minerva Press

LUNE IT

Hallucinatory stories from East Kilbride... Please do not judge it by the cover too much.

For Mariele

Full Moon Bloom

1

An artist stood back, dripping paintbrush in his left hand, and scanned the newly painted bluey green swirled archway, admiring his work. Vincent's turbulent nature compelled him to look around for further appreciation. His audience looked up amazed at the fact that this strange man could perform such a task so quickly and painlessly in such cruel weather. 'Full power!' was all they could reply, teeth and eyes gleaming in the bright sunshine. The artist's goofy grin fell as he was brushed aside by a swarm of paranoid looking party animals and a tall rakish-looking woman who steamed up the path, eager to escape from the searing heat. Vincent called after their leader, a ghostly figure whose shaven headed, porcelain complexion made him look like he had just returned from the spirit world, 'Have some respect man,' he cried in a stoned drawl, 'I'm a fucking artist.'

'I don't give a shit about your scribbling!' sneered the party baba. 'I'm just trying to get out of this hell.' His friends' expressions voiced their disapproval at Vincent's disrespect for their guru, before escaping into the cool shade of the hotel lobby.

The hotel proprietor, a hawkish looking twenty-five thousand year old, forced a quick smile at the oncoming spectacle before ushering in his guests and barking an order to his servant to bring in a round of chai.

It was just ten hours before the first night of a new moon and the local travelling fraternity, an ethnic gumbo made up of people from everywhere who'd recently landed in the sleepy Far Eastern town, had begun to awaken from the narcosis inspired by the previous month's festivities and prepare for another celebration of the sentient madness of their existence. Pravan was quietly amused by the sudden attentiveness of the roving party heads but also pleased at the opportunity to make a good deal of money and increase his power within the local community. The skeletal man was making it clear what he wanted doing and was becoming quite irate at his host's painfully relaxed attitude to the whole affair. 'Today we must have *full power*. No shanti, you understand,' he patronised, sweat pouring off his brow. Pravan shrugged, 'Please, don't worry my friend, tonight will run like a cool breeze,' he said, lying back in his threadbare seat and taking in a cool blast from the overhead fan. The baba masked his annoyance, grabbing the tail of a nearby lizard and flicking it out of the door without a second glance. The tall woman had sat through such conversations a thousand times before so decided to brave a conversation with the moody painter outside.

'You see this lady,' whispered Vincent to the young Siva standing next to him. 'She's a very nice woman, a bit fucked up, but nice.' Siva could not understand a word of what Vincent was saying, but smiled anyway as the woman strode towards them, tie-dyed skirt and long red hair billowing in the breeze.

'Hi, I'm Vanessa, I've just returned from the mountains... What are you doing here?'

'What am I doing here? I don't know, what are you doing here?' he frowned. 'Do you like my painting? Look, can you see it?' he gently put his arm round her shoulder and pointed up towards the swirling lines which at the top of the arch gave the impression that they were leading beyond.

Vanessa lost herself for a moment and had to steady herself against the wall. 'Wow!' was all she could utter.

'See, I told you,' winked Vincent to his young friend. 'I want to paint a butterfly too – up there I think,' he continued, pointing up to the balcony. Vanessa followed his gaze and had to sit down. The butterfly was already there.

'Are you going to the party tonight?' she asked, eager to go off at a tangent.

'Of course!' he replied. 'It's the only reason I came back to this place. I've been living in Pishanga, up in the hills, painting. The people up there are fucking crazy, they don't know anything. I'm like a king!' He raised his arms as his ego inflated. Vanessa was not impressed and took a swig of soda, looking back up the path towards her friends.

'I still haven't decided whether I'm going yet. I got beaten up by the police last time. I can't take that kind of karma – you know what I'm saying?' she frowned.

'You shouldn't worry about such things,' he said in a brotherly way. 'Those fucking bastards don't know anything about this. Pravan's using someone's land up in the mountains. Those fucking guys will never even find us.'

Vanessa stood up again, warmed by this overdose of confidence. She smiled hazily at the painter, before being swept off her feet down the walkway as her friends stormed through hungry to return to their chillums and air-conditioning.

The young traveller broke his brief meditation as the crowd brushed past him. 'That hat looks shit my friend,' said one of them as he walked by. Ola shrugged and continued shielding his eyes from the harsh rays of mid-afternoon sun which reflected off the whitewashed walls of the hotel with an incandescent brilliance.

'What is their problem?' he said as he passed Vincent.

'Oh, they're just hot, you know what I mean,' he laughed. 'You are coming tonight, aren't you?' he added seriously. 'It's not good to miss a party for dead people.'

2

Ola's girlfriend Helena had been feeling nauseous for days and did not want to go out, which pissed him off. Beautiful women were everywhere, his lingum was going haywire. He'd resorted to eating charas to kill off the temptation.

'Helena? Helena!' he whispered, jogging her shoulder and tugging her earlobe with his teeth.

Helena murmured 'Mmm!' and turned over before the ache in her stomach kicked in. 'It hurts Ola... Find a saddhu for me, he'll get you some opium,' she said lazily.

Ola ignored her and went outside. The last two months away from his home world had seriously messed around with his body chemistry and his present situation was making him feel quite powerful, immortal even. He didn't have a clue what he was doing, and he liked it.

Leaving Helena to go back to sleep, he wove his way through the patchwork garden and up a winding staircase to the flat roof above, his shadow growing long and sharp beneath him as the sun sank below the green and yellow mountains in the distance.

Ola could hear Pravan's children playing games on the unfinished patio. His wife, a beautifully sculpted saried princess, smiled as he followed his shadow to the top of the stairs. The children stopped playing. Pravan's oldest daughter, a golden eyed six year old, stared at him in a mysterious silence which unnerved him considerably. He felt like an alien invader all of a sudden and decided to sit down.

Staring out over the horizon, the traveller listened to the wailing mantras and drum beats which emanated from the multitude of temples which littered the region. His eyes were being assaulted by the sunset, a hauntingly beautiful confusion of green, orange and purple shades, which stood magnificently behind the hills and muddled collection of flat roofed dwellings and pale blue-washed minarets. The young Siva joined his guest, who had started to freak out, and greatly appreciated the company. Siva's eyes sparkled gleefully as he pointed into the near distance.

'Look! It's Munrat. He does this every evening – nobody knows why.'

Ola looked round to see a strange dancing man on a rooftop some thirty yards away, blissfully unaware of his seemingly possessed actions.

The traveller wondered at the spectacle for some time, until his concentration was broken by a blast of techno music that ripped through the air. Siva had disappeared down a passageway.

'Mendek! Hey! Mendek! Where the fuck are you?' Vincent's unmistakable stoned drawl projected from the garden below. 'Come down man, let's get some chow.'

Ola peered over the balcony, greeted by his strange friend's wiry black hair and lobster red from the sun face. He drifted back to his room, kissed Helena long and darkly on her parted lips, and followed the hyperactive artist back out into the world. He was not totally elated at the prospect of spending another evening with Vincent and without his lover, but what could he do? At least it wouldn't be boring.

'Look at me,' called Vincent. 'I'm tall just like you. Where do you want to eat?'

'Venus, let's go to Venus!'

The green neon 'Venus Restaurant' sign glowed in front of them. Ola swept away the vines that shrouded the entrance and loafed in.

The Venus restaurant, unlike Venus, was decidedly green. The neon lit the long marble tables and illuminated the customers in its healthy aura. Ola and Vincent sat at a table amid a throng of expectant party goers and glanced at the new moon, which shone through the leaves above like a cool blue diamond.

Vincent started to chatter away to a friend opposite, and Ola was left with the prospect of breaking into a conversation – but had no need to.

'What are you doing here?' asked a hard-faced woman of indeterminate age, rather critically.

Looking into her bright green eyes, he gulped before speaking, 'I was hungry so I thought I might get something to eat. My name's Ola.'

'He thinks. Shit,' she quipped to her friend before continuing her conversation in a tongue he could not understand.

'*E forno,*' stated her friend, looking at him idly over her shoulder.

Vincent had sparked up the joint he'd been carrying behind his ear and passed it to him casually. 'Those crazy gypsy women are not for you,' he laughed. 'You go with them and you'll end up in the mountains somewhere talking like an idiot.' He pulled a face as he received their scorn and cried, 'Keep away from me, you crazy bitch! I don't want your kind of magic.'

The crowded restaurant was silenced briefly. Vincent accepted the frowns and amused stares and laughed out loud, before greeting the old man who brought out their food. Ola scanned the scene around him, marvelling at the abundance of wildly clothed figures and luminously painted faces. He was struck by the beauty of a shaven headed girl who stood under a yew in a sparkling white sari, chattering excitedly with her two male companions. Like lions they loved the spectacle before them, criticising it with a subtle artistry.

'Who is the laughing man,' she mused, looking towards Vincent. 'He looks like a happy devil.'

The taller of her two companions tweaked his finely crafted beard vainly and answered with an all-knowing authority, 'He's Vincent. He comes out at night from the darkest reaches of hell to confuse us. You should try him.'

Samara 'Mmm'd' in agreement and affectionately bit his ear as he coolly pulled away, continuing, 'I spent last night smoking with him. I still don't know who the fuck he is. He's not even here, he's like some cartoon.'

'A genuine flying tortured soul,' sang Eddie, the beauty's other companion, lazily picking at his guitar.

'Let's do some acid!' she said excitedly. 'We can double up later and trip through until the sun comes up.'

She pulled a small sheet of paper from between her breasts and placed two tabs on her friends' tongues. Eddie continued to play his dreamy melody as he swallowed, and Yuri accepted a long kiss from Samara. Ola looked up at the stars.

3

Pravan and his brother, after finishing their quiet family dinner, strolled to the edge of town to join the convoy of beaten up old buses, mopeds and cars that would take them up into the hills. The elder brother was beginning to enjoy basking in his ego. Coping with these interplanetary revellers was no mean feat and he wanted everyone to know it. Siva was happy to watch his brother take in the locals' feigned applause while he stood quietly by. A new lunar cycle was of great significance to them both; their days of celebrating it in the far away desert temple had ended long ago. As youngsters they'd never imagined that the full moon could be so lucrative. How could these rich travellers find it so central and important to their lives? Siva listened inattentively to his brother's ramblings and tried to work out the significance of a dream he'd had the night before.

He'd been sleeping on his roof, under the stars as usual. In his dream he saw the faces of several village chieftains spinning above him, shouting down at him angrily. He was petrified but powerless to wake up, silently screaming out in his sleep as the images shattered and fell through space like shards of silver. He'd asked Ola what it might have meant, but his new brother was too dazed to answer.

The latter's smiling face met them as they turned the corner. He'd tried to follow the mysterious woman he'd seen in the restaurant, but lost her in the crowd, and was now wandering the streets trying to find the jump off point for the party.

'Wow! Pravan! Siva! Do you know where we're going? I'm so lost I was about to give up and go home,' he said.

'Please don't worry my friend,' replied Pravan. 'Come along with us.'

Siva grinned. 'Full power!'

Three streets later and they were met by the sound of coughing engines and clouds of leaded pollution. Pravan jumped into a jeep, which soon sped off in a cloud of dust and exhaust. Ola spied Vincent entertaining a crowd of smiling locals, and padded towards him.

'Ahh! Mendek,' he cried as Ola approached him. 'You see this guy? He's got no mind at all – you know what I'm saying?' he addressed the crowd.

Ola grinned back while he thought of something to say, but his mind was blank, so he laughed it off. His eye caught a glimmer of bright white material appear and disappear into the fumes. The party baba emerged from a nearby jeep, anxious to get away. The driver sounded his horn.

'Are you coming or what? Get in man,' he ordered Ola who, startled at the new attention, piled on in. 'Here, hold these.' He handed the traveller a cloth bag. 'It's the music,' he said. 'Guard it with your life.'

The young driver looked about twelve. He looked around and smiled saying, 'Tiger raja.'

Vincent and four others clambered in, and the vehicle creaked off out of the smoke and into the darkness.

4

Ola was not happy with this kind of pressure. The life and soul of a party was in his hands, as he clung on to the roll bar of the jeep which bounced along the pitted country road with one headlight, at indeterminate speed.

'I like your space ship,' said Vincent to the driver. 'Where can I get one?'

The driver didn't answer, letting the passengers enjoy the journey and the relative silence. The party baba stared grimly ahead of him. Two more months in this dreamstate and he could return to his wife back on their home planet. All around them was complete darkness. He thanked the creator that he'd let the cosmos shine through.

The young driver turned the wheel sharply, almost instinctively, and the vehicle leaned over and headed down a steep slope, towards a collection of dim lights on the horizon.

5

'So we have established contact with the red planet,' the sample stated mysteriously from the PA system which sat in an alcove of a shallow gully, sending the electronic sound waves bouncing around the hillside. Vincent, sitting under a tarpaulin, grinned baring all his teeth and howled wildly at the moon above, as a scantily clad woman swept past, eyes and teeth gleaming violet under the UV beam. She wailed with glee, jumping into a crowd of hypnotised others. Karma streaked faces and wild eyes met Ola as he gradually became caught up in the menacing rhythm structures. His feelings had gone beyond fear and into grounded flight. Everyone was in a state of panic because they couldn't take off. Maybe that's where their enjoyment came from, deep within their selves. Or was it just the moon? He was on the edge of the mad circle. Ola looked up at the sky and fell over, as Pravan lit another array of fireworks which scored into the sky. Samara, catching another rush, span out through the crowd into a stream of white sparks that burst from the ground. Unaware of any danger, the mooners ran in and out of the streams, wailing like banshees. Their faces became blurry, merging together before re-emerging as a totally different body. The dancers gyrated as one with the bass line, the wind in the trees and each other. Their expressions seemed to suggest they were somewhere between pain and ecstasy.

Ola was spinning out. His stars were all shooting at the same time, and he soared back out into hyperspace. As he pounded into the earth, Samara span around in front of him. She glared at him and licked her lips. He had no qualms about being her next meal, but she span off as quickly as she'd arrived.

Siva sat quietly in a full lotus position and watched. From the far side of the gully he could just make out four battered, unassuming figures walk calmly into the throng. As they drew closer, another firework fired off up into the moon, showering the dancers in coloured light. The four figures then broke into a lazy jog, then a run. Siva could see they were totally oblivious to the sounds and sights surrounding them, their eyes were focused on him, he could not understand why but let the apprehension wash over him. They were obviously wired into their selves and a dark mystical knowledge. Some thirty feet away and they paired off, swooping towards him, each pair holding hands, their eyes burning like hot coals. Siva tried to move but could not help but sink into a warm paralysis, as the four figures let their feet leave the ground, they glided towards him, two of them clutched his shoulders and carried him away.

6

Ola saw the ghostly figures float off into the night sky, but in his mind it was just a trick of the light. His ecstasy was immense, and he howled with his new friends at the moon.

Samara was contemplating his future over a glass of chai with Vincent. 'I'm flying south next month, but I don't want to go alone,' she said. 'This man has not really travelled before, so he should go with me.'

'Then take him,' replied Vincent. 'Civilisation has made him weak, you could take him anywhere. He's fascinated by you. Look at the way he's dancing, totally tuned. The guy's a potential superman!'

'Easy baba,' she replied. 'I want to sleep with him first. *You* know what I am saying.'

Vincent laughed and gave her a hearty slap on the back, sending her flying back into the confusion. She wanted to dance for ever, but the sun was creeping over the horizon and she had to catch a life before floating into another cycle. Ola, blissfully unaware of her intentions, was dancing with his back to her.

Samara ran up behind him and gently pinched him saying, 'Come with me, it's different outside.'

Ola turned, his eyes sparkling as the rest of the planet spun around. She opened her mouth slightly and he stuck his long tongue down her throat. She pulled back, grabbed his hand, trying to pull him away with her.

'Where are we going?' he shouted.

'Do you really give a shit?' was all she would say, and he followed her into the dawn.

Ola awoke with a start to find himself alone on his back in a newly ploughed field. The morning had brought the dew out. He was soaked and empty inside. Was he dead? He couldn't summon the energy to find out. Instead, the traveller stared on into pale blue space as the sun caught up with his field of vision.

'Fuck, I can't remember anything,' he whispered. 'And I'm naked.'

Ola turned over on to his stomach. Looking ahead of him he saw the lithe torso of Samara, gaily skipping towards him chewing an apple, unafraid of her nakedness.

'Do you want some?' she asked, bending down in front of him. 'Isn't this great? We're starting again.'

7

Vincent drained the bottle of mineral water and threw the empty container into the scrub, as was the custom in those parts. Lack of sleep was making him irritable and worried about his future. He needed a blessing. Clasping both hands together in prayer, he smiled weakly as a red robed priest washing himself down at the lake looked at him calmly, before immersing his head in the brown murky waters. Vincent solemnly asked for his blessing, and knelt at the waters edge, as the priest muttered an unintelligible assortment of incantations, sprinkling the tall stranger in the muddy liquid. Vincent looked down into the lake and calmly watched the filth and excrement float by. Local myth stated that the lake had been there since the beginning of time, and was the source of all creativity. He wasn't totally sure about that, but he needed the illusion; to let him know where he was at more than anything.

The holy man placed his hand gently on Vincent's fore-head, saying, 'Baba, you're a lucky man cause some trouble,' before taking a silver coin from the man's open hand and returning to his puja.

Soul cleansed and relishing the compliment Vincent bounced back up the steps towards the hotel. It was that great time when the world had just started to get up. Floating down the main street, the artist happily observed the cows waking up, as the pig population rolled around in the filth. Taking a bunch of bananas from his knapsack, he placed them next to the head of a sleeping leper, feeling guilty and angered that his magical powers were so pitiful.

Vincent hated reminiscence. The fine line he walked could not afford such frivolities. But he couldn't help reliving the image of Ola disappearing into the darkness, helplessly caught up in Samara's wild world. He laughed into the sky, and then cursed as he slipped in a fresh mound of shit.

'Fucking animals,' he muttered, eager to get back into trouble.

Helena opened her eyes, staring momentarily up at the graffiti fractal on the ceiling. It was kind of traditional in these cheap hotels to do your bit and try out some creativity. She didn't like this one though. Fractals never did much for her, they didn't go anywhere. Spreading her arms out, she realised Ola had not returned. 'Bastardo,' she thought, 'leaving me like that for some hippy orgy.' She leant over and sparked a roach from a beside ashtray. Her dysentery was gone, today she would have a good meal and go exploring. Where in hell was Ola?

Vincent had reached the stage between exhaustion and wide awakeness, a kind of lackadaisical madness. Returning to the hotel, he heard Helena singing to herself in the shower. He waited for her to come out.

'Oh! Vincent, it's you,' said Helena, trying to hide her disappointment. 'Where is Ola?'

She tied a blue towel around her damp blonde hair and faced Vincent, bare breasted, eyes flaring. The way he looked at her made her feel a great sense of exposure, aloneness even. She sat down, and suffered the moments of silence before Vincent spoke.

'When you travel, it's easy to go off on tangents. A new moon can do marvellous things to your perceptions. You shouldn't feel so attached to just one life. Explore your own fate. You shouldn't think too much about time and home, you're always at home.'

Helena listened, but could not come to terms with what this man was saying. She felt warm and cold inside, like a mercury.

'Ola's grown up now, he can look after himself. You are not owned by him. He may be gone two or three days even, I have a motor bike, we're friends aren't we? Let me show you Pishanga, it's my village.'

'Fuck Pishanga, I'm not going anywhere with you. I want to get some opium, it'll chill me out until Ola comes home... Look I'm sorry, I'm just worried, that's all. Come on, it's too hot to go up into the mountains. Do some opium with me,' she beamed, surprised at how quickly she'd recovered her enthusiasms.

Vincent, totally unfazed, agreed wholeheartedly. He received her apologetic kiss and they headed off towards Naga's house.

'Do you know this man?' asked Helena. 'Naga – isn't that a snake god who lives in the desert?'

'What's in a name? Naga can get crazy sometimes, but he knows how to treat his guests. Besides, you're with an artist, what could possibly go wrong?'

'I have a curious nature, that's all.'

'Curiosity... That's important. You should test yourself every day, or you turn into these people,' he said disdainfully, waving his big hand towards a huge pot-bellied vendor who sat in his shop drinking chai, surrounded by hundreds of cardboard boxes. 'This life is not for us.'

'Yeah,' replied Helena dreamily, following Vincent up a steep flight of stairs into Naga's house.

'You'll like this place,' Vincent whispered. 'Naga lives in a strange and beautiful world.'

They entered a room carpeted with ancient, finely woven rugs. The walls were lined with silken paintings of beatific deities and shelves lined with ornate wooden and stone sculptures. Naga lay on his back in a pile of oversized cushions, singing lullabies to his companion, a dark skinned woman who lay comatose beside him. Seeing Vincent and Helena walk in he raised his head dreamily and smiled.

'Vincent my friend, it has been so long. Who is this special woman you've brought to see me?'

Helena flushed and introduced herself, extending her hand. He took it and leant over as if to kiss it as an aristocrat would, but instead grabbed hold of it tightly and pulled her down into the soft cushions surrounding them. Vincent celebrated the spectacle with laughter, and lay down beside the sleeping beauty, who remained in her dreams. Helena, slightly startled, edged away.

'Please, don't be afraid of me, I cannot stand formalities. I saw the moment you walked in that we would be friends. Everything I have is yours; we are on the same journey,' assured Naga, rubbing the sleep from his eyes.

'Helena has been ill,' informed Vincent. 'She's feeling better this morning but would like to leave her body for a while.'

Naga smiled knowingly, 'I feel this way myself sometimes.' He reached out behind him and took a silver jewel encrusted pitcher from the shelf above. 'Vincent, please. Pass me those goblets. Are you going on this magic carpet with us?'

He could see the apprehension on Helena's face, and took some offence. 'I'm a good swami. An inner journey will do you good. If you don't like me you can leave.'

Naga's eyes looked deep into Helena's soul, she met his gaze, but could not look into his face for long, so took the goblet from his hand and took a sip of the rich syrupy liquid. Naga downed his and drifting back into the abundance of cushions, let the goblet slide out of his hand.

8

Helena listened to the hypnotic raga notes that poured through the window from a record player far away. Vincent and the dark skinned woman lay sleeping. As Naga nonchalantly stroked her smooth unmarked belly with his long fingernails, she stirred in ecstasy.

'What is her name?' asked Helena.

'Her name? I really don't know,' answered Naga. 'She has many dark secrets. Talking is not her pleasure, you know what I mean?'

'No, not really.'

'The tongue is a very curious instrument and very few people have the power to control it. Your tune can save you or land you in shit, it's as simple as that. This woman has decided to explore higher forms of communication. That is why she spends so much time in the world of dreams. Come with me on to the roof, I have something to show you.'

Helena followed, too enthralled to argue. She sat with Naga in a lotus position and looked out on to the world. A very different one, in fact, from the one she'd just come from. The sky, instead of blue, was here of a deep purple complexion. Its dark light, however, did not affect the brightness of the land below. The mountains had regressed into a volcanic past and shot rainbow rivers into the stratosphere. The town was now shimmering white and as yet there was still no sound. Helena sat with her mouth open.

'Close it,' ordered Naga calmly. 'Don't let the evil fly in. Hold my hand; we can levitate here. It's easy.'

He hummed like a lazy bee, and off they hovered over the roof, down into the streets below. The roads were not solid; they were more like coloured ether which swirled around their ankles, carrying them forward into a blinding platinum temple structure, where Helena met the people of this new planet for the first time. The forms were basically human, but their skins were painted in a myriad of spectral colours. Their lack of clothing seemed unimportant. She looked into the face of a woman floating by. Her age was ambiguous; she could have been anything from twenty to twenty thousand years old, the deep lines in her face etched with seams of silver. An orange tear welled up in Helena's eye as she saw the peace and inner beauty in the woman's face. She tried to speak, but no sound emerged. Instead, only wisps of blue smoke mingled with the thin clouds already dancing around. Feeling immense joy well up inside her, her body felt as light as the ether surrounding her and she let herself float towards the purple colours above. Naga reached out to bring her back, but she'd decided where she wanted to go. He wouldn't follow. The temple had no roof and she floated skyward, towards a crowd of white-faced winged spirits. She beamed at them, but they had no mouths and their eyes span like kaleido-scopes. Helena looked down, but the landscape had disappeared. She was trapped in this purple haze with her new kaleidoscopic friends. The spirit holding her hand sensed her fear. He drew a finger in front of his face which extended like a bright spark, one hundred miles into the sky. He whipped his arm back in a circular motion, ripping the purple space open like a curtain.

The spirits disappeared into the new white cloudy sky, allowing Helena to float to earth with the graceful ease of a feather. Helena blinked, and opening her eyes again, she felt the cool breeze of the fan overhead and the buzz of a fly in her ear. Whisking it away she inadvertently hit Naga, awakening him from his deep slumber. The latter twitched and awoke with a start, then lay rigid for a moment before smiling at Helena. She relaxed, and let him kiss her gently on the mouth.

'I have to go up north, into the mountains. It's more business than pleasure, but it's a good trip. You should come with me. I would like it very much,' he tempted.

Helena contemplated the idea for a moment, Ola leaving her like that had displeased her intensely. He had always teased her about her lack of adventurous spirit, so going wild like this would certainly put him back in his place. She agreed.

'I would like to come very much, but first I must return to my room and get some stuff together.'

'That place can give you nothing. Trust me you will go without nothing,' he replied, with a hint of authority in his voice, which worried her slightly – but did not put her off.

She put her head through the hole of the warm camel-haired poncho, and eased on to Naga's revving motorcycle. It was evening, but the narrow streets of the town were still humming with life. He accelerated, leaving a trail of dust in his wake, and his companion clasped her hands around his hard stomach for dear life. Insects and flying winged beasties of all kinds buzzed around in the bike's headlamp as Naga wove in and out of the traffic, human and animal alike. Passing a street vendor's stall the biker reached out with his left hand, plucking a bunch of grapes from under the nose of the napping store keeper. He howled with delight at his stunt, plucking several off before handing them back to Helena, who was beginning to get a thrill from the rush of adrenaline. She let the grape juice run down her neck, flinging the remains down some dark alley as they flew by.

'Helena!' he shouted over the roaring engine. 'How do you like being a phantom?'

By now the town was far behind and they roared silently into the hills. For Helena, the experience was akin to travelling in a time machine; the past was being swallowed up behind her. She turned her head to look back. There was nothing. In front was the future. The solitary headlight shone into it, painting the dark shadowy world, before it died behind them as quickly as it came.

The roads were becoming steeper and more treacherous; the roads in this part of the country were full of potholes and the roadside unbarricaded. Helena could just make out the jagged pattern that marked the fine line between the surface and the spatial nothingness beyond.

'There is a hotel in the next valley. We stop there for the night,' shouted Naga.

Helena could not understand how he could read the darkness with such accuracy, but she had no intention of questioning him. She lay her head in is hair, smelling the acquired aroma of hash, suddenly realising that she wanted to fly into the tomorrow.

Naga skidded to a stop outside the Shamski lodge, an isolated collection of bungalows, backing into the mountainside. The two riders let the clouds of dust settle around them and Naga brushed the dust off his clothes with a grimace. Removing his shades made him look like a panda, which made Helena laugh out loud. Her companion grinned until he worked out the joke, and wiped the black sediment from his cheeks and forehead. Now her wild companion looked like a white tiger, rare and unfathomable. She loved him.

They walked majestically into the hotel lobby, where a middle-aged concierge lay sleeping.

'Hello! Friend!' called Naga.

The unconscious man gave no reply.

'Perhaps he's dead,' whispered Helena, with a crazed mixture of excitement and apprehension, to Naga, who grinned before leaning over to tweak the man's ear. The concierge awoke with a start, taking a moment to regain his composure.

'Naga! How very good to see you again. This time, I see you've brought some pleasant company with you. You may be pleased to take room number three, I think.'

'You think right, Hamed... The key if you please,' answered Naga, already bored with the man's sycophancy.

Taking the rusty door key, Naga and Helena walked back outside and along the gravel path, arm in arm, and happy at the fact that they'd fuck each other into the tomorrow.

The morning sun blazed through the opened window, singeing Naga's face. He turned over into Helena's chest, immersing himself in her shadow. She awoke and kissed his forehead, then his eyes and nose. He remained motionless.

'How far is there to go?' she asked.

'Not far,' he replied. 'We'll stay here until night fall maybe. Pass my bag over, will you. I need a chillums.'

Day flew into night, and into day again, until Helena couldn't remember what she was doing there in the first place. She knew being this relaxed wasn't at all healthy, but she really didn't want to do anything about it. The air-conditioning cooled them down. They were both happy to watch the room spin around.

The fourth day of their stay at the Shamski Lodge came and went. That night when darkness fell, Naga hauled himself out of bed saying, 'It's time. Let's go.'

'Don't worry about paying, he doesn't give a shit. I'm his cousin,' he drawled as the bike sped on mercilessly eating up the road ahead.

9

This second night journey was pretty much the same as the first; black mostly, with the odd streak of light. That was until a police check point loomed up in the distance, striped pole barricade separating the earth from the horizon.

Naga eased to a halt and whispered to Helena nervously, 'Don't worry about this guy, he's nothing. Just smile sweetly. Nothing's going to happen.'

He removed his shades and looked the officer straight in the face. The latter did not move from his seat. Helena was not sure if he was able to. The man returned Naga's stare. He was in no hurry to let them through. It had been a long night, where little had happened and he wanted someone to torment for a while. The officer chewed off a fingernail and spat it out in their general direction.

'Where are you going?' he began, as he picked his nose, rolling the gummy snot in between his thumb and forefinger, giving Naga one of those demon headmaster glares.

'I'm taking my girlfriend here up into the mountains towards Hajo. Do you know it?' answered Naga, as Helena tried her best to smile sweetly at the policeman, unimpressed by the small revolver he'd begun to stroke in his black leather holster. He did not answer Naga, preferring to gloat over his companion in a blatant misuse of power. Naga was getting twitchy, 'We're just tourists,' he continued. 'I realise we've put you through some trouble. Perhaps I could give you something for your time?'

'What would I want from a shit like you?' the officer replied without averting his gaze from Helena. 'I have the weapon, you do penance for me. Stay there and shut up, okay? You, the woman!' he said raising his head. 'Come here and sit on my lap. It's lonely out here at night, you know. Show a little charity to your local law enforcement officer.'

Helena looked at Naga for help, whose stare had now locked in on the man in front. 'If you take that back I might give you a tip, okay friend. Don't make me feel sorry for you, okay friend?'

The officer hauled himself up out of his wooden chair, taking the gun out of his holster and prodding Naga with it, who turned away; more because of the fact that he couldn't stand the stench of stale spirit on his breath than the apparent peril he'd put himself in. He turned back and met the officer's glare. The latter already coming out of his stupor, and sensing his own abstract danger, digressed. He laughed and patted Naga on the shoulder, in a vain attempt to pass the incident off as a joke.

'No hard feelings uh? Give me your ring and you can go through, no questions asked. I have a wife and eleven children, you understand. I have a right to piss people off.' He chuckled weakly and held out his hand to shake on the deal.

Naga took the hand and gripped it hard, his face filling with malice as he peered into the guy's soul, 'You know what. I wouldn't give you a germ.'

He slowly shook the man's hand, keeping him in his vice like grip. The officer's knees buckled and he fell to the ground, unable to take the flow of energy passing through him. He dropped his weapon and looked up at Naga who, seeing the pleading and submission in his eyes, let go. The other passed out and lay frozen in stasis.

'Is he dead?' asked Helena, peering over the near rigid body.

'No, just detached for a while. Some of these guys just don't know how to treat a human being. He's had a long night, he deserves to be turned off for a while,' he said, all too matter of factly. He turned and kissed her. 'I'm sorry. He must have been quite an embarrassment for you. Sometimes I just can't take living with the male condition. Come on, let's go. Hajo's not far away.'

10

Heavy rain had fallen the night before Naga and Helena's arrival in the tiny mountain village, leaving the blue green grass fresh looking. The dew covered its surface like shattered glass. The wooden houses looked ancient, like the gnarled trees scattered around. It was the sort of place which made you feel spaced out. Helena screwed up her eyes, as the sun peered over the jagged mountain peaks.

'Why is this place called Hajo?' she asked.

'What? Hell, I don't know. Come on, I want to introduce you to some friends of mine. I think maybe you'll like them a lot, they're very spatial. Kind of techno pagans, wired into an abstract third-age cyberworld. They're quite wary of meeting people in the flesh. Just remember to take your shoes off before you go in – and don't swear, for fuck's sake.'

Helena smiled and walked through the open doorway. The ground floor appeared empty, until she saw four or five black Siamese cats run like ink drops across the floor. The walls were lit by stripes of UV light.

'Maybe you'll want to keep your sunglasses on for this bit,' whispered Naga. 'They should be upstairs.'

He tiptoed playfully to the foot of the staircase, holding Helena's hand. It was spiral and automated, like an old world escalator and painlessly drew them up into the third floor.

The room there was huge like a loft extension. The window frames were rhombus shaped and the shuttered light shining through created snake like patterns on the floor. The other light was unnatural, emanating from orange bulbs and an impressive collection of lava lamps. Helena felt like she'd just walked into a dried out aquarium. 'Wow!' was all she could say. Naga's friends were huddled closely around a large monitor, fiddling around with all manner of keyboards and hardware gadgetry. So intense was their concentration that they did not notice the two new arrivals.

'What mischief are you up to now?' Naga called out, grabbing their attention.

The three dreadlocked orange robed cyberjunkies turned around lazily and grinned, before continuing with their work. The tallest, Gedge, spoke first.

'It's the magic man kids. Maybe you'll stay longer this time; maybe we can change the world. And you've brought a friend. That's great, five is a powerful number. Risky, but powerful. Please come and join us.'

Gedge's two companions grinned and made a space. Dark, ambient music hummed from a spherical speaker. Helena and Naga knelt on a fish-shaped inflatable, anxious to see what, was going to happen next. Helena could not help but giggle.

'Do you want some drugs?' asked Naga openly.

'We've stopped,' said Uma, a cherry-faced female Buddha, with a hint of pride.

'Well, almost,' added Gedge. 'We've been making our own, using ancient Aztec recipes – all totally organic of course – they're great. We haven't slept for three weeks.' He looked at Helena, his eyes wide like whirlpools. She remembered her dream, and felt a cool spurt of adrenaline.

'I'd love to try some,' asked Naga excitedly.

'Of course,' cried Uma, 'there's enough for everyone!'

She passed him an oblong glass bowl full of small, col-oured miniature potato-like objects, dyed in all different colours. Helena picked one up and peered at it closely, as Naga took a handful, stuffing them down his throat.

'We thought that if they were colourful, the effects would be more interesting,' said Uma.

Naga ignored her completely, letting his excitement and impatience overtake him. Eager to get into this new game he asked gleefully, 'Okay let's do it. How can we conquer the world?'

'Change the world, Naga, who'd want to conquer it?' said Uma. 'Imagine the world is a soft, foamy ball, sitting quietly in the palm of your hand. The harder you squeeze, the longer it takes to return to its original shape. Do you understand what I'm saying?'

'No, not at all. What's next?' he replied.

Gedge interrupted, 'You're very lucky Naga. You and Helena have come at a very exciting time.' He was apparently oblivious to the fact that Helena was now rolling around the floor in hysterics. Gedge, however, remained earnest. 'You may not know this yet, but thousands of satellites are spinning around our planet, transmitting television signals and messages at the speed of light, to homes just like ours. Some of these satellites are more specific, and are used by rich first world governments to spy on their rivals. The people in control of these machines are unaware that they're invading peoples lives, watching them fall apart. They have no intention of doing anything about it. It is their form of entertainment.'

Helena sat up, her curiosity aroused. 'I've heard about people like this. What can we do about it?'

'That's what I'm getting at,' he said intensely. 'Please be patient with me; we have so much time.' Helena listened in awe, as Naga started playing with some gadgets. 'These people are the same ones who control the flow of information. They believe they can tell *us* what is right and wrong. We have found a quick and painless way to burst their bubble.'

'Yoga powers are useful, but hold no influence in their world. That's why my operations are more on the ground level, you understand. Cybernetics is the only way to cure the pigs upstairs,' interrupted Naga, taking another handful of coloured potato pills.

Uma continued where Gedge left off. 'By using this new technology, we've discovered that these satellites are constantly renewed. They can't be bothered to take the new one out of orbit so they're just left flying around up there in space with nothing to do. We can key into their circuitry and play with them ourselves. Watch this.'

Helena didn't have a clue about what she was saying, but the way she said it made it sound pretty fucking exciting. Uma and Gedge began playing with oscillators and typing data into keyboards with the speed of experienced secretaries. Pike, the third guy in this band, had disappeared. Returning with a camcorder, he calmly began to record the proceedings.

'Yes!' cried Gedge. 'We've keyed into satellite Presley!'

The huge monitor in front of them crackled. Helena jumped as a printer next to her switched itself on, and began to feed out reams of data in Esperanto and binary, the spewing paper fed back into a laser scanner, which translated the information into a language a human could understand.

'We'll be on line in twelve hours,' informed Uma.

'On line to where?' asked Naga, disappointed that there hadn't been any fireworks.

'Ahaa!' cried Gedge. 'We'll be on-line to Potslovia. What do you want to do next?'

'I know,' said Helena, 'let's meditate.'

The five revolutionaries agreed. Leaving the computers to do their stuff, they headed outside into the bright sunshine and sat in a circle on the coarse grass. Uma sighed as she made pictures out of the thin stratos clouds above.

'Do you know the "Shine your psychic light from a star" technique?' asked Helena.

'No,' replied Naga. 'But I know you can teach it to us.'

The five sat in lotus positions and closed their eyes, listening for Helena's instructions.

'Take in a deep breath. Fill your lung capacity and let go, gently, like you're blowing a bubble to a far away place. You feel relaxed and calm, and you should feel happy. Think about the place you're in and the friends around you.' This repetition lasted for some minutes, then she continued. 'Now you are sitting on a star, far away from our world. You watch it as it sits calmly, silently, in space. Now look at the faces of your friends and your family; all the people you care about. The light you shine from this far away star reflects on to their world and brightens their future.'

The five were feeling warm and very peaceful. A tear welled up under Pike's eyelid. He remained motionless as it trickled down his face.

'Your world is at peace. Let yourself float gently from the star, back into the world and reality... The end.'

They opened their eyes and sat in silence for a few minutes, flushed and smiling.

'Wow,' began Naga. 'That's a good meditation, I like it a lot. It makes me feel good inside. Powerful but in a nice way, useful even. Wow, I'm feeling pretty spaced.'

'Gedge! Uma! Pike!' called a booming voice from a neighbouring house. 'If you are not busy, I would like to invite you and your friends to my home this night for good eating and conversation.'

'It's Ramaman. He used to be a chef to a king some-where, I don't know where. But he gets all these amazing foods from all over the world, he cooks them to perfection,' informed Uma. 'Shall we go?'

'Definitely,' replied Naga, licking his lips like a hungry lion. 'Let's smoke a chillum. I need to work up an appetite.'

11

Wearing baggy green pyjama bottoms and hooded kaftans borrowed from Pike's wardrobe, Helena and Naga followed the three cyberjunkies towards Ramaman's huge wooden house on the horizon, as dusk fell. The clouds of fireflies and midges came out to play, dancing chaotically with each other in the warm evening air.

'You see that star up there?' said Uma to Naga. 'It's my star. I found it over a year ago now. It's called Jelly Beluga.'

'Really?' he replied. 'I'll race you there. I'm hungry.' They raced off, pants and kaftans flying in the wind.

Ramaman welcomed his guests with open arms. 'Good evening to you my friends. Please, feel free in my home.'

He ushered them in, like a royal butler on Prozac, into the banqueting hall. The huge room must have been thirty metres in length at least. Silken mandala wheels lined the walls, some fairly new and others more ancient, to the extent that the colouring had cracked and darkened with age. Helena looked around, suitably impressed. After taking off her sandals she enjoyed the thick woollen shag pile under her feet, letting Ramaman's collection of marsupial pets potter around in their own little worlds. She turned to face her host, who wrapped her in his huge hairy arms placing a firm kiss on her forehead.

'Who is this beautiful child you've brought to see me, Uma? Her eyes are sparkling with new life.'

Helena smiled and blushed at the same time, overwhelmed by his compliments. She took his hand, as he led them to their seats at the long oval banqueting table. The seats were made with firm styrofoam, and moulded perfectly into the shape of the arse of the person who sat in them.

'We have brought you a gift Ramaman. See.' Uma opened a velvet pouch, bringing out a handful of red herb. 'It's red saffron, the best in the world. I know how you need it.'

'You're an angel!' he boomed. 'How did the gods ever let you down here?'

Gedge and Pike frowned at the statement. This man cooked great food, but was always totally annihilated. They watched him observantly as he glided out of the room and into his kitchen, shouting, 'Music! Please!'

One of the mandalas rolled itself up, revealing a sixty inch television screen, which showed a spinning giant green purple fractal. Eclectic electronic music whispered around the room. Naga, sitting at the head of the table, stared into it taking lungfuls of the exotic aromas which spread from the kitchen behind him. Helena looked in his direction as he stared towards her vacantly. She hardly knew this man. The fractal reminded her of her hotel room, but primarily of Ola. Her anger towards him had virtually gone, and she'd begun to miss him terribly. She tried to suppress the feeling of fear and exposure which had begun to well within her.

'Do you feel all right? You've gone all white,' asked Pike and Gedge, in perfect synchronicity.

Helena's eyes rolled up into the back of her head and she fell backwards, passing out into the thick carpet underneath.

12

Helena opened her eyes, on to a thick starry canopy, as a distant sun shot across the sky. She shuddered, as her left ear was licked and nuzzled by one of Ramaman's wombats. Since her mild panic attack, the meal had come and been consumed with great relish by everyone else. Especially Naga, who was now chewing on a big cigar, blowing chubby smoke rings into the sky. He grinned at her, as she shooed away the furry beast from the chaise lounge where she lay.

'Helena? Helena, what happened? You were doing so well. A stranger is supposed to pass out after the meal, not before it. You'll have to stay for one more night. It's customary.'

She sensed a hint of disdain on Naga's face. Ramaman looked most offended. 'One more night. What are you talking about?' she tried, but no words came out, only gasps.

'We can read your thoughts, my dear,' said Uma, who'd just walked out on to the veranda. 'Running backwards is not an option we can afford. The knowledge you possess may be of great use and value to someone else. You know what I'm saying?'

Helena nodded and drifted off. The dreams she dreamt were dark. Mostly shapes and figures darted around in front of her, like animated slate etchings. Suddenly, a ghostly mirror image of herself appeared in front of her. It stared at her curiously before opening its mouth, spurting out streams of rainbow colours, which then exploded into millions of tiny fragments, reconfiguring into an image of her lost love. Ola smiled briefly, but his eyes looked sad, the pupils dilating to the extent that no colour in the iris remained. The blackness she looked into glittered, and she realised the new reflections were hundreds of reflections of herself, gleaming white and naked, spinning around in front of her. She desperately wanted to wake up. She struggled with herself for a while before doing so, on a black mahogany four poster water bed, in a red velvet paper room, perspiring profusely. She wiped her brow on the black satin sheets, and thanked her creator that it was Naga lying fast awake next to her.

'Good afternoon. You're becoming a regular Ms Winkle. Why do you keep flaking out on us like that? You're missing some really great food. Come on, let's go back. Gedge tells me we're on line to make some mischief,' he smiled.

Pike, Uma and Gedge were hard at work with their keys and switches. They were now in control of satellite George, who was almost in position, four hundred and fifty kilometres above the republic of Potslovia.

Pike spoke excitedly, 'Five... Four... Three... Two... One... Satellite Presley is on-line!'

The TV screen remained in static for a moment, before crackling. It then revealed a telephoto view, some fifty or so metres above the enclosed circular cobblestone courtyard of a reconstruction of a medieval castle. Uma zoomed in closer and sharpened up the tracking. Five bodyguards patrolled the walls with heavy looking automatic weapons. Three men and an old woman stood under a tarpaulin balcony, and looked over at the grim scene in the courtyard below. Uma zoomed in briefly on the third man, freezing the frame briefly.

'This man is Oren Forks, the president, king and military leader of Potslovia. This is what he likes to do on a Saturday afternoon after morning prayers. His private life has been a closely guarded secret up until now. We've only heard stories filtered through, from travellers who've met refugees and exiles from his country, about what he enjoys; you know what I'm saying? If these images are what we expect, we could bring down his whole international support system and topple his dictatorship.'

She pressed another button, and the spectacle continued. A small portcullis opened inside the courtyard, whereupon several animals padded out warily. From what Naga could make out they were cats. Not wild; more domesticated. Helena looked on expectantly. Two metal chutes slid down from the top of the walls, into the courtyard. A man appeared behind the figures in the enclosure with a large steel bucket. He carefully tilted the bucket into the chute. Dozens of tiny writhing black shapes fell out, and skidded down the chute into the courtyard.

'What are they?' asked Helena, still trying to figure out what was going on.

'They're mice, I think,' replied Naga, and the other three nodded in agreement.

As the tiny creatures tumbled on to the gravel below, the cats stopped padding and licking each other. They tensed up for a second, before pouncing on the new arrivals, performing the massacre with cool clinical precision. The mice tried to run, but they had nowhere to go. Some froze in panic, awaiting a quick death. The cats playfully flung their prey into the air, before shaking them to death as they sat helplessly in their mouths. The observers watched the spectacle idly, as if it was a regular event, conferring calmly as the insides and body parts were flung in all directions. Uma and her guests sat in front of the screen, unable to say anything. Gedge got up swiftly and ran from the room. The others heard him puking up the previous night's meal into the toilet next door. Uma decided to speak; she couldn't bear to prolong the shocked silence.

'This, this *monster* has the lives of over twenty six million people in the palm of his hand. He owns two nuclear power stations, twelve satellites and ninety five percent of the land. He must be stopped.'

She held her head in her hands and wept, as a wolf entered the arena. Its ribs poked through its matted grey hair, and its teeth bared into a snarling grimace as it prowled. The cats by now had finished their meal and were basking in the sun, licking their fur. Those who saw the wolf enter first arched their backs, hissing in fear and anger at his presence. The wolf, insane with hunger, began attacking his prey. Uma opened her fingers and dared to peek out through her hands. Helena clung on to Naga for support. The wolf continued his slaughter, oblivious to the fact that the cats, outnumbering him completely, were fighting back, tearing into his flesh with their claws. From the balcony, Oren asked the old woman next to him to pull a metal level. She did so. Black ooze poured out of some drainpipes, into the courtyard below. The battle continued, as the black syrupy liquid covered the gravel. The cats and wolf began skidding in it, their fur becoming increasingly soiled and matted in the blackness. Oren lit a candle from his seat in the balcony and threw it coolly into the scene below, smiling with his two companions. The far away observers stared in horror as the candle landed in the black stuff, engulfing the animals in a moment in a sheet of raging hellfire. Oren Forks and his minions left the scene as smoke began belching up. Soon the clouds grew, to the extent that the whole view from the satellite was shrouded in blackness.

'For fuck's sake!' Naga exclaimed, and wandered outside on to the balcony, eager to get some air.

'I realise this man is a complete psychopath and he should be buried, but he's so far away,' said Helena, still suitably distressed.

Naga returned to the room, smoking a joint, as Gedge came back from the bathroom, wiping his face with a red towel. Without speaking, the three returned to their keyboards and started typing again.

Helena's face was drained of colour. 'Helena,' whispered Naga gently, taking her hand in his, 'they still have a lot of work to do. Come with me outside.'

She agreed, and they took the spiralling escalator down-stairs, and walked barefoot out on the waving grass.

The jagged peaks loomed violet and purple far away. Naga and Helena walked until the houses were out of sight, and lay down together under a tree, beside a fast flowing stream. Naga leaned over, sinking his face into the clear waters. Helena stared at the horizon.

Naga gasped as he pulled up out of the stream, his thick black hair dripping wet. 'Have you ever been to Jibberwarah?' he asked. 'It's a peninsula down on the west coast. You can swim with the dolphins this time of year, if you're lucky. Hajo's great, but it can get a bit intense, if you get my drift, and if I eat any more of Ramaman's food I'll never leave. You know what I'm saying?'

Helena was surprised at how shanti he'd become. He caressed her thighs, and she leant over to kiss him. The two undressed each other and played in the stream, until the setting sun painted the rippling waters orange and black, like the skin of a tiger.

Gedge and his two techno friends sat through into the next morning, working with the intensity of the mosquitoes that buzzed around them through the night, while Helena and Naga supplied them with endless streams of chai and herbalisms. The sun and moon passed each other by once again before their work was done.

'That's it for now in Potslovia,' cried Gedge, allowing his ego to get the better of him, as Pike resumed capturing the moment on video.

Uma continued, 'The footage we captured from Presley has been copied and beamed into media controlled satellite communication systems spinning in our orbit. The images we saw are now being witnessed by TV and cable stations all over the planet.'

'It's been a long time,' said Gedge. 'Let's go to sleep for a while.'

The five embraced each other, kissed, and retired to the rooftop, where they slept like lions under the stars.

13

Naga and Helena tiptoed out, leaving the other three to enjoy their dreamless sleep, and sped off in search of sea and dolphins. Naga was pleased to have caught up with some old friends, but was now in intense concentration as he steered his machine down a thin track through a virgin forest. The bike and its riders were now caked in thick brown mud, which sprayed around them from the rain filled puddles that had sprung up in the previous night of heavy weather.

Soon the forest thinned, making way for ploughed land and paddy fields. The landscape was strangely devoid of people. Everything was still and taking care of itself. The scenery changed once more, the land becoming barren and infertile. Now even the grass thinned and made way for desert, first sandy dark yellow rocks and then rolling sand dunes. All the bikers left behind them was a cloud of dust. Naga was feeling totally relaxed and in tune with his cycle, rolling with the bike to avoid the pits and troughs in his way. He focused in on the horizon and gazed as a caravan of camel riders crossed the desert, kilometres away, their silhouettes blurred but unmistakable.

'They must be heading for the oasis,' he thought. 'Shit, I hope they're not arseholes. These people either love you or kill you.'

He was right; the caravan reached the oasis a short time before they did. As Naga pulled up, the desert traders had unloaded their camels, and were quenching their thirst in the still waters of the desert oasis. Their skins were the colour of dark honey, stained by months of hard outdoor travel. As Naga and Helena approached, they were eyed suspiciously. One of the band, a crimson robed giant, walked towards them, barring their way to the water hole. Naga was unimpressed and continued forward. The giant desert man shook off his crimson hood and strengthened his stance, pulling out a thick twelve inch crooked dagger from under his cloak saying, 'This place is not for you. We have travelled great distances to get here. You and your woman will carry on.'

'Carry on? What kind of foolishness is this? The oasis is a gift from the gods. They will be angry if you refuse to let two fellow travellers go and quench their thirst,' replied Naga.

'What do you know of the will of the gods? I have dreamt of this meeting. Only evil will come of it.'

'My friend, did you know the word evil is live when turned around? I and my companion are travelling a thin line also. Let us rest.' Naga ripped a silver chain from around his neck and handed it to the giant man.

The latter sheathed his dagger and took the gift, smiling. '"Live" I had never thought of it in such a way. It puts forward the question of when is a life good? When it is dead? I hope not. I like to think now that it is maybe only men who are evil in this world. But our evil stems from our addiction to women. This is why I spend my life walking with the gods through these dunes. I digress. You may stay with us, if it's only for one night.'

Helena, utterly confused by what had been said, and amazed at the fact that the man could string a sentence together at all, smiled quickly before rushing down to the water's edge with Naga to take a long cool gulp of water. Her mouth was as dry as the sand surrounding her, and she'd always found the whole bullshit male domination trip a waste of time and air space.

'These guys are fucking gone,' said Naga excitedly. 'Sun struck, inner space out of here nowists. You're gonna hear some real mad shit tonight.'

'Oh really?' Helena replied.

★

'What are your names, if you don't mind me asking?' asked Helena openly to the camel men, who were now sitting in circular formation around a charcoal campfire.

'Our names shall remain a secret,' replied one of them, surprised that she'd even opened her mouth. 'Knowing someone's name can be very dangerous. Knowledge like that can give a scheming man control of someone's soul. We prefer to talk in concepts rather than lives. Do you understand?'

'Then spin me a concept, my friend,' cried Naga, eager to let his mind run wild.

'The concept of a sphere,' said one of them, rolling a berry around with his tongue.

'Wow!' said Naga, laying back and looking up at the stars.

'I have a concept especially for you,' said the giant to Helena, who listened expectantly. 'The concept of leaving your friend here to play with his machine and returning with me to my harem.'

Helena let the concept sink in and backed away. The camel men hooted with laughter, holding their sides to stop them splitting, reliving their humour with vigour, letting Helena wonder whether it was humour at all. And if it wasn't, what would living in a harem really be like?

'Please don't believe us too much,' he cried. 'We are all very small here. There are more stars and galaxies in the sky than grains of sand in this desert. Trust me, harem life is not for you. Though your friend here might make a good eunuch.' He repeated the sentence in a different tongue, and once more they suffered their own hysteria.

'What did I tell you?' whispered Naga. 'More than one night of this, and we'll be just like them.'

Helena remained pensive until she drifted into sleep.

14

Leaving Helena and Naga far behind, the camel riding conceptualists had long since disappeared into the dunes by the time their new biker friends had awoken into the searing heat of their current desert reality. Eager to escape into a slipstream, the two revved up their engines, and continued towards a rendezvous with the dolphins in Jibberwarah.

'You will like today, I guarantee it. Swimming with these animals is like swimming with the gods. You'll feel like a mermaid!' cried Naga.

Helena lost his words as they sped by, but appreciated their intention, and squeezed her companion as he negotiated the winding paths that curled through the desert wildness like a giant sidewinder. She imagined what it would be like swimming with such animals. She'd wanted to be a mermaid since her childhood. Helena stopped thinking, letting the air rip through her. For the first time, her world was singing to her. She listened.

Jibberwarah stood as Naga said, upon a broad peninsula. It had been a whaling town until about fifty years previously and the population made a living out of the ritual slaughter of fellow mammals until the nobler beasts were killed off completely or just wised up and stopped coming back – nobody was quite sure. But the population, disillusioned that their creator stopped their supply of food, migrated to other parts of the country, leaving Jibberwarah to crumble into the ghost town it now was. A collection of fifty or so unimpressive dwellings, now crumbling through age and lack of attention, rusty harpoons, whale bones, half sunken long boats, tumbleweed, engine parts and a thriving lizard and cat community were all that remained. Helena was as yet unimpressed. Naga sensed this and broke the impression with a healthy dose of enthusiasm.

'I give you Jibberwarah! A haunted town, but still a town. Home of oceanic phantoms and sea monsters. I know it's shit, but our underwater friends live over the edge out of sight. It has been just two years since their return. The hunters know they can never come back. They're under a seventy year curse for their crimes against nature. Condemned to a life inland, where the sea is out of sight and they work with the earth. Come, the diving suits are this way.'

Helena peered out into the calm blue ocean, as she followed Naga into a derelict fisherman's cottage. He kicked away a threadbare rug from the sandy floorboards, and lifted up the trapdoor underneath. They shielded their eyes from the tiny dust devils that swirled around. It was hard to imagine that such a place could have been someone's home. She felt a twinge of sadness, as she saw a decrepit painting of a whale hunting scene hang crooked over the mantelpiece, and a moth-eaten rag doll sitting charred and forgotten in the tiny fire grate below. Naga disappeared down into the darkness, cursing as he tripped over some inanimate object.

'Helena? Can you find me a candle or something? I can't see shit down here.'

She scouted around the empty house. Finding a dented rusty oil lamp, half full of oil, she lit it and followed him down into the musty smelling cellar.

'How did you find out about this place?' she asked, as she and Naga swept the dust off the oxygen cylinders and jumble of diving equipment.

'A marine historian friend of mine from way back was doing some research here for his thesis. He stashed some diving gear here two years ago and said I should drop in if I was ever in the area. He didn't really want many people to know about it, you know. We didn't want the whalers to come back; they'd give our underwater buddies too much trouble,' he laughed. 'Come on; help me haul this stuff down to the jetty.'

Helena dangled her flippered feet over the old wooden jetty as Naga adjusted her equipment. 'It might sound dangerous, but it's not really. You just have to breathe. The current's nothing to worry about. Just give me a nudge if you see any sharks... Look!'

He pointed directly ahead towards a school of some seven or eight bottlenosed dolphins, jumping in and out of the waves like dolphins do. Helena held on to her pang of excitement, and looked at her companion wide-eyed. Naga grinned.

'We've come just in time. These guys are playing here until the monsoon season, then they follow the Gulf Stream south. They're beautiful animals. The natives along the coast think they're immortal and live in a kingdom far beneath the waves, with the whales and merpeople.' He took her hand, and they both rolled into the waves.

The underwater kingdom around the jetty was littered with trash which the whalers had discarded all those years ago. The iron harpoons and engine parts were now corroded, almost beyond recognition, and lying in the sandy beds made foundations for the mussels and sea anemones to live. The divers swam through the tepid waters, weaving in and out of the slimy rock formations in search of the dolphins. The fish population was sparse, but decidedly varied, and showed no desire to swim with these new arrivals. Clouds of silver scored through the waters, in search of smaller food. Helena looked down into the sand and seaweed, watching the crabs and other bed life go about their business. She could get used to this world of no sound and all action. They had dived deeper now, the light becoming less available. Naga signalled her to stop as he spied something glittering far below. She waited as he satisfied his curiosity. A big fish with huge eyes appeared out of the darkness, eyeing her up, before it returned to the blueness. Helena turned sharply, startled by a sharp upshot of bubbles that emanated from Naga's direction. She was confused, but knew she could not afford to panic. Her fear had since become an overwhelming sense of pain and loss. The bubbles ceased, and were followed by a dark cloud of liquid, like blood. Helena's petrifaction prevented her from moving. She could do nothing but fear the worst for her friend, as his lifeless torso floated past her, towards the surface. Legs and left arm missing, the other clutching a shiny metal object as if his life had depended on it, Naga's death face looked down on her as he floated upward, a white mask of pain and disillusionment. Helena watched helplessly as three striped sharks rushed past her, eager to finish off their prey. Her whole self gripped in cold panic, she swam back towards the jetty, too horrified to look back.

The sun set and disappeared over the edge of the world, before Helena could summon herself to move. She had been lying on her back since her return, trying to come to terms with the fact that her world with this strange man she hardly knew was shattered, and she now found herself stranded in a country she didn't understand without the knowledge or means to rediscover her former life. Helena's state of panic had induced her into a state of hallucination. Looking up at the stars, she saw the two faces of her past, those of Ola and Naga, spinning around inside and outside of her head. Eventually, she pulled up into a foetal position, and tried to rock herself into a clearer mind state. The moon was beginning to pass through another cycle and looking up at its unfinished shape, she felt even more cold and hollow inside. Its light, though, gave her a view of the ocean, its waters now choppy and more menacing than those of the previous afternoon. Rummaging in Naga's cloth sack, she dropped two tabs of diazepam, and knocked herself through into tomorrow.

The morning, with its harsh light and unforgiving heat, had left Helena falling down and had made her realise she would have to evil her way home, wherever that might be.

15

The concept of starting again with Samara was as appealing as his current situation; that of nakedness and a bed of stony soil. Samara stood over him, her impressive figure blocking out the sun like an organic colossus. Ola was speechless, still thinking that the whole scene was a dream, or even better a joke. Yes a joke, that would be great. His clothes would be hidden behind a tree in the next field and he could return to his hotel with a smile on his face, no one would be any the wiser. Samara probed his mouth with her blackened toe playfully.

'Come on, we've got a whole world to ourselves. What do you want to do with it? You are a god-man, aren't you?'

Ola shied away, his head spinning with fear and confusion. Samara turned, and danced away into the bushes. He pulled himself up and followed, hoping she'd lead him to his clothes. Shit, Helena would be going frantic. Samara gaily led the traveller down a slope, towards a vast expanse of unploughed land. He grabbed a branch from the scrub to cover himself. The lovely Samara looked back and frowned, slightly exasperated at his bashfulness. The landscape was unpopulated, save our two travellers. Ola could do nothing but follow. Any evidence of the previous night's party had disappeared. Catching up with her, feet bleeding and lungs out of breath, he pulled her back, anxious for a few moments of sane communication.

'Look, think there may have been some mistake. I'm really not cut out for this running naked through the forest bullshit. I'd be really grateful if you could tell me how I can get back to Allopuzza,' he said, gripping her hand with some urgency.

Samara pulled away sharply, unimpressed by his demands. 'You are something of a disappointment, aren't you. You can't just party with me and leave.' Her eyes glowed with anger. This is what starting again is like. If you can't hack it, then fuck off. I'm going over the mountain to see a holy man. If you stick around, you might learn something.'

Ola, seeing her spirit outweigh him considerably, could do nothing but tag along like a lost child.

Samara's holy man lived in a small mountain co-operative, which merrily span clothes for the nearby towns, and prided itself on telling mysterious stories to anyone who could be bothered to listen. The dozen or so villagers stopped their work, and stared in a mixture of amusement and astonishment, as the scantily clad pair approached. Samara strode through the free range chickens that clucked around, straight into the circular hut, which stood at the centre of the village. Ola followed her in, noticing the thin stream of smoke that worked its way up into the sky through the wooden chimney before he entered.

A man of indeterminate age sat cross-legged in meditation, chanting in quiet monotony. Samara ordered her companion to sit down. He did so and they waited. The man after several minutes slowly opened his eyes and tilted his head in Samara's direction. The rest of his skinny body remaining motionless, as he spoke in a deep lyrical voice.

'Samara. Your beauty shines more than ever today. I trust you celebrated the new moon with your usual enthusiasm. I am pleasantly surprised. I haven't had any visitors for over five moons. Does your man know how to make a chillum?' he asked, without looking in the young man's direction. Ola, already feeling positively microscopic, decided to improvise. He shakily began cleaning the holy man's twelve inch brass chillum, which lay ceremoniously on an old velvet cushion beside him, and continued to fill the instrument with a charas and dry tobacco concoction. The pipe was then handed back to the holy man, who clasped it in his hands, signalling to Samara to ignite it with a crooked branch, which sat smouldering on the small fire.

She did so, leaving the holy man to fill his lungs with an abundance of the acrid smelling smoke. As he did so, the top end of the chillum glowed, and sent bright orange sparks singing around the hut. He then exhaled, letting his two visitors look on, as the room was consumed by a fog of greeny grey fumes.

'Boom! Molin art,' stated the man, in a voice deeper than thunder. Samara stared on in wonder, as the pipe was passed in an anticlockwise direction towards her. The ceremony continued until the smouldering chillum died. The holy man proceeded to knock the ashes into his fire and stared at them with great interest, before booming, 'Samara. Samara's companion. Your future looks fast... Fast, but colourful.' Samara took the thought seriously, as Ola went green and fled the room.

'Your friend is very new,' he said. 'Maybe you should leave him with me for a short while. I will give you some clothes, and you may continue your journey. If you like, you may collect him in... two, no, three months. Bring me something next time you visit, in trade, shall we say... I'll make a god out of this civilian for you.'

The two drowned in each other's eyes, before resuming a state of transcendental meditation, as Ola returned, unaware of the strange new future that awaited him.

16

Samara, newly attired in purple pyjamas and a green and red poncho, crept silently out of the modified wigwam and out into the cold dawn, leaving her holy friend and her disappointment behind her. She hated goodbyes. Being barefoot made her walk faster, especially as the ground had been made colder overnight by a healthy dose of frost. She hurried down the winding mountain path into the next valley, where she hailed a passing bus to take her on to her next destination.

The ageing machine struggled to negotiate the snakelike roads as the few passengers clung on to the seats which had begun to pull away from the floor, making the ride infinitely more uncomfortable. Samara tried her best to ride with the bumps and jolts, whilst returning the gossip and looks offered to her by the other passengers with beaming smiles. She didn't know where she was going, but it was a long way from Potslovia.

A short time passed and the bus stopped outside a small town, where a family of some eight children and three parents climbed on. Samara was warmed by their laughter and excitement at the prospect the bus journey. The children each carried their own water containers and paper sachets of food for the trip. Their adult companions were hauling what seemed to be their life possessions, including a crate full of angry chickens and an evil looking goat, which made its best attempt to escape from the vehicle before conceding and taking a shit on the floor, prompting the children to squeal with delight. Samara laughed with them, wishing she could be that young and innocent again. They argued and fought like all good kids do, remarking at the scenery with a shared fascination. Samara's attention was attracted to the smallest, a young girl of about six or seven who looked knowingly in her direction and smiled. This warmed Samara's soul to the extent that she let the tears roll down her face, remembering that she could never have a child of her own. The young girl saw her pain and cried in empathy.

The light was fading, scattering the shadows inside the bus. Samara huddled up with the children, to keep warm through the cold night, and ate a mango before suffering a bumpy sleep through into the tomorrow.

Surprised at her ability to sleep at all in such conditions, Samara slipped away into a dream. She remained on the bus but here there were no passengers and no seats. Instead there were cushions, hundreds of them, flying around her in zero gravity. Outside there was nothing but bright white light and a multitude of coloured stars. Wow – her dreaming had achieved an entrance into a fifth dimensional technicoloured space. She flew forward to talk to the driver. The unshaven, feni-soaked drunkard from her conscious state was now replaced by the holy man from the mountains, who sat, arms behind his head, driving the vehicle with his mind. He turned as she entered the cabin, cocked his head to one side like a curious cat and blew a cloud of blue dust into her face. Samara sneezed back in his face, which had now turned into Vincent who'd begun to paint his face orange and black. The paint emanated not from a paintbrush but from under his long curling fingernails. Looking out of the throbbing purple windscreen, the timespace traveller watched her bus rotate three hundred and fifty degrees and fly as if through hyperspace into a cluster of blue stars, which melted together into a spinning peacock fractal. Vincent smiled.

'You've completed your mission baby. We're bringing you home.'

17

Opening her green–blue eyes, Samara found herself soaking up the evening sun on a red lizard chair, overlooking an ultraviolet lake of water and ether. She listened to the singing voices of children that pierced the thin veil of mist. Naga sat beside her, smoking a golden bejewelled chillum and blowing thick smoke rings across into the ether. Eddie and Yuri swayed into the soft rhythms created by the young Siva, who sat levitating above a lotus flower, playing on his imaginary flute. Red and green notes floated out of his heart into the sky, where they were eaten lazily by a passing herd of winged dragons. Samara decided to leave her chair and move closer to the hypnotic music, but the silk binds around her feet and hands prevented her from doing so. She was momentarily confused, but felt no pain. Seeing her friends tied in the same way relieved her confusion and returned her to a calm state.

Naga continued to send smoke signal, idly watching them as they floated above their prison idyll. The four flying mystics who'd carried Siva away appeared again, and soared through one of Naga's smoke rings. Landing simultaneously, the four were silver-faced and wearing black. They shook their heads and smiled, unimpressed by their guests' laziness. Standing as rigid as statues the four materialised into separate atoms, reconfiguring again into one form, a golden-suited platinum-skinned superbeing of indeterminate origin. With a wave of his hand, the being dissolved the silken bindings that fastened them. Opening the palms of his huge hands, he willed a miniature sphere into each of them. His left hand held a golden sun, and the other a moon. The guests gathered closer, peering into the spinning orbs, and seeing the two new worlds of Helena and Ola in each. Helena was wild and seething with energy in the sun, and Ola moody and disillusioned in the moon with the mountain holy man.

'I know how you love to play games with these inno-cents,' he began in a cool melting voice, 'but these games are not allowed. Acts like these warrant a lifetime in Potslovia. However, your imaginations please me. You will return to your planet and work back instead. Naga and Samara smiled sheepishly like naughty children, as they were carried through the ether. Naga to Ola's place in the mountains and Samara to the jetty in Jibberwarah.

Ola clenched his teeth and Helena wailed in ecstasy, as the two travellers achieved a simultaneous orgasm, to the delighted amusement of Pravan, who sat listening from his chair in the hotel lobby. He stubbed out his joint, and decided to brave the heat of day to search for his missing brother. It had happened before; his little brother spent so much time in a state of semi-consciousness that he would disappear, sometimes for several lifetimes. It peeved him slightly, because it left him with all the pressure of running the hotel on his own. Reaching the end of the path he pondered a few moments, before hanging a right to Naga's house. He hadn't seen the elusive crooked pillar of the community for some time and felt he owed him a visit. Perhaps his lazy brother was hiding there.

Much to his bemusement, neither Siva nor Naga were in residence. The latter's room full of curios was now inhabited by Vincent who sat, with the confidence of a king, on the pile of cushions, dreamily stroking the hair of Naga's comatose maiden friend.

'Pravan. Hello. You wouldn't believe this girl – she's amazing. She's in a perpetual state of sleep. She sleeps, sleep walks, eats and drinks. Look, watch this,' said Vincent, utterly fascinated.

He reached out and plucked a small phial of potent smelling liquid from the shelf beside him. Opening it up, he waved it under the nose of the sleeping dark-haired beauty who quickly stirred, becoming more and more aroused by the flowery aroma. Vincent gazed at her intensely as he pulled the phial away from her, drawing her out of her horizontal position, then swaying the little container from side to side. The woman followed, as if under a spell of deep hypnosis.

'You are in my *power*,' exclaimed Vincent cheekily, before falling back into the cushions, creasing up in hysteria. Pravan looked on, trying to stifle a yawn before speaking.

'Have you seen my brother anywhere?'

'No, he's not in here. Come, we will go in search of him. I need an adventure,' he said, jumping out of his seat and into the bustling streets below.

'Pravan my friend,' said Vincent as he strolled along the dusty main street, smoking a tobacco leaf, 'I love your town. Every day there is something new. You never get bored. I am finding it very tempting to stay here, you know, and buy a small place and sell my paintings, marry that sleeping beauty.'

Pravan pretended to listen as he scanned the area looking for his brother.

'Pravan! Vincent!' called out a painter from his tiny shop cum gallery, tucked away down a side street. 'Take some chai with me. We have much to talk about.'

They willingly obliged, Pravan taking a seat beside his artist friend as Vincent wandered inside to investigate.

'Pravan, it has been many moons since your last visit,' he began, patting his friend on the back. 'Tell me what has been happening in your story.'

Pravan relaxed and the two talked about their business, family, dreams, et cetera. Dimitri was a strange but good man, working hard through the day to support his family, saving his immoralities for the night time, when he explored his needs and desires within the privacy of candlelight and shadow. He showed Pravan his most recent work, a piece painted on parchment in gold and silver lacquer. It was a surreal image portraying two wild-haired painted dancers spinning around, their arms outstretched under the full moon. Pravan remembered his last party, letting Dimitri know that he was suitably impressed, as his eye caught sight of a familiar silhouette limping towards them. Naga forced a smile as he approached. He looked terrible, as if he had just returned from a season in hell. Clothes torn and ragged, and face burnt by the sun to the extent that he'd begun to blister, his complexion had become mottled like that of a leopard.

'Hello... Pravan, Dimitri,' he said, trying to hide a grimace.

'What happened to you, man?' asked Dimitri, always enthralled by someone else's adventures.

'I really couldn't tell you my friend. All I know is that I feel like shit – and someone's stolen my fucking motorcycle. Please excuse me, I'm needing to go down to the lake for a bathe.' He waved to Vincent and the two others, before disappearing in the fashion in which he'd arrived.

Pravan and Dimitri waited for him to turn the corner before bursting into laughter.

'That is a strange and terrible man. Too fucking wild. He makes me happy to stay at home in bed with my wife,' laughed Pravan.

Vincent called out from inside, 'Pravan, he's here! I've found him for you.'

Pravan walked in, as Dimitri returned with great concentration to his painting. Pravan was as yet confused by what Vincent had been saying. The big man was crouched down in the far corner of the shop peering at something which lay in an old dusty suitcase. Pravan stepped carefully over the piles of artwork that were strewn around. He sat down beside Vincent who was now smiling beatifically.

'What is it?' he asked.

'Look!' he replied, holding up a glass painting. It was a coloured portrait of Pravan's lost brother, smiling like a buddha, surrounded by a beautiful long-haired woman and an abundance of lotus flowers, under a starry purple sky.

Surfing Insanity

1

Saul strode towards the cracked concrete kerb as it glistened a yellow orange in the raindrops under the street lamp. Taking a swift glance to his right he closed his eyes, swallowed his apprehension and stepped out into the road.

Immediately, adrenaline began surging through his veins, his mind's eye portraying a fragmented view to the other side and super fear spurring him on. Three steps and a car swept behind him, the slipstream sending the long coat-tails of his black raincoat flying around him like a Dracula cape. Ignoring the car's horn and the driver's unintelligible expletive, Saul pressed on. Two more steps and he felt a large hand grip his shoulder and pull him down hard into the pavement on the other side. Saul awoke with a start and looked to his right, seeing a black Jaguar scream into the horizon.

'Death by Jaguar!' he exclaimed in awe, contemplating the idea for a moment before looking over at his assailant, who'd just picked himself up off the damp pavement and grimaced slightly as he brushed the muck and grime from his bright orange trousers.

'Just looking out for you, man,' he beamed.

Saul didn't answer; he was glaring at a middle aged woman, who had been staring at him in petrified amazement, quite overcome by the unexpected spectacle, her fallen groceries rolling slowly across the paving stones and into the gutter.

'Yes?' he yowled at her from the pavement in his thick Scottish accent. 'What do you want?'

Picking himself up off of the ground, he followed Agent Orange into a bar as the woman hurried home.

The Phoenix bar was empty, apart from a solitary Guinness drinker sitting on his own and looking pensive in a threadbare crimson armchair beside an uncleaned yellow nicotine stained window. An attractive but heavily made up barmaid stood, arms folded, behind the beaten up old bar, transfixed by the flickering light of a television that glowed in a corner. Sean sat in another, puffing away at a roll-up next to a ghost, whose painfully short attention span was torn between the TV set and Aden's energetic monologue. His normally unhappy expression broke into a wide crack in the sky grin as he spied the entrance of Saul and Agent Orange, who swept through the doorway and glided towards them, fondly remembering them from a previous life.

'This guy was just centimetres away from being flattened to a pulp by some arse in a Jaguar—'

'Zen crossing the road,' interrupted Saul with uncommon glee, smiling at the ghost as he did so with a crazed glint in his eye.

The four greeted each other, before the two new arrivals hurried off to get a drink. The barmaid dragged her attention away from the television as Saul and Orange approached. The latter smiled at her, wiping a damp ginger dreadlock from his face, then instinctively looked across the pumps to see what was on offer.

Saul eyed the barmaid fiercely, straight in the eye, booming 'Whisky!' and proceeded to light up an oversized cigarette. 'And no ice,' he continued sharply.

The barmaid smiled weakly and turned towards the optics. Understandably, she felt somewhat disturbed by Saul's imposing presence. Aside from the fact that he stood at six feet eight inches and weighed in at well over thirteen stones, he carried grim reaper businessman like persona. Crowds seeing him perform pyrotechnics at festivals around the countryside to the tortured sound of Iron Butterfly recordings witnessed an awesomely surreal spectacle. Some of his public believed him to be an incarnation of the devil himself.

Orange swaggered back to the table, a foaming pint in his left hand and a perturbed expression on his face.

'That barmaid's fucking miserable,' he said.

'I wouldn't worry about it,' replied Aden. 'She's like it with everyone. Something to do with perpetual premenstrual tension.'

'How could you know that?'

Aden beamed.

'You've shagged her haven't you? Fucking sex maniac,' stated Orange as Aden laughed, taking the insult as a compliment, and taking another swig of his pint.

'It's true my friend,' continued Aden, turning to the ghost. 'Total sex addict, nymphomaniac, heaven's prisoner. Three women on three consecutive nights this week, and fucking loving it. Falling in love on a regular basis is like tripping, dream reality.'

'You are a moral vacuum, sir,' cried Orange, in a pompous aristocrat impersonation. 'One night stands are like stag nights; you wake up the next morning not knowing where the fuck you are or what you're doing there.'

Aden rose to the challenge with good humoured bravado, replying, 'Morality is a pre-Woodstock phenomenon, sir; an unnecessary framework constructed by religious institutionalism in collusion with the governing powers, with an aim to keep its audience in stalemate. Besides, I like not knowing where the fuck I am when I wake up in the morning – it's great. There's no good or bad experience, only karma.'

The two agreed to disagree – but threw their fags at each other anyway. The sparks flew, the Guinness drinker muttered disapprovingly from his corner and the ghost laughed silently into his glass.

Saul on the other hand remained impassive. After a mere ten minutes in the bar he was growing restless. That afternoon he'd made a special effort to closet his usual misanthropy and leave his castle to face the crowd. This was partly due to the fact that Orange was in town. He was a sorcerer and someone you just had to meet to believe – as was Aden his apprentice and the ghost, who was a freak in most senses of the word, and rarely failed to act as a source of alternative medicine. His lost tortured nature was so apparent that you could not help but feel good about your present situation whilst in his presence.

But this day the ghost's mind was somewhere else. He wasn't working and Orange and Aden's sex orientated conversation put him in a mind to leave. His own sexual history came to an abrupt end at the tender age of eleven, after an eye-opening encounter with a school French assistant and a garlic crusher. He now preferred to explore darker, less conventional turn-ons. He'd recently adopted a native belief that sex was merely one of several forms of death that one could pass through in his life; the others including imprisonment, working on a regular basis and his own preferred 'walking into death' variety. He sighed cigarette smoke across the table, glaring disapprovingly at the ghost's inattention.

The latter awoke from semi-consciousness, staring back at Saul fearlessly and beginning, 'Aden tells me your family originated from India.'

'Yes, but only my father's side. He is a Sikh, from Amritsar,' answered Saul proudly, more than happy to talk about himself for a change.

'Sikhs... They're good people. Very strong,' answered the ghost reticently.

Saul smiled, his self suddenly coming alive again. 'I'm going to become a saddhu and walk through India; you know, totally free!'

The ghost, having recently returned from an eight month trip to Saul's home planet, was still feeling decidedly spaced out, his perceptions knocked out of whack. He had drunk more than his fair share of bhang lassis, and returning home was something he happily refused to contemplate. Having left his soul, amongst other things, on the subcontinent, he was more than happy to get back there, even if only in conversation.

'A saddhu, hmm,' he continued. 'They're pretty extreme people, very difficult initiations. You'd have to sit for three days without moving, totally covered in ash.'

'No problem,' answered Saul without hesitation.

'And eat your own faeces.'

Saul looked at the ghost, slightly taken aback by his new knowledge, but replying, 'Hell, yes,' anyway.

'I met one in Andhyra Pradesh; well he was more of a fakir really, an old drug smuggler who thought their way of life could get him ahead. Most paranoid guy I've ever met.'

The three others at the table becoming quickly bored with the ghost's reticences took a tangent and rushed to the bar for some more alcohol. Saul scowled, and the ghost, disappointed by the lack of interest in his experience, returned to the television.

2

'I'm going to save your night!' cried Aden to the ghost, picking up a green porcelain ashtray from their table and throwing it into the television set. His spontaneous action was so quick, that the now crowded bar was immediately thrown into confusion. Nobody but Aden, the ghost, Orange and Saul had a clue how this window into another world had been smashed. Whilst some of the customers stood around in shocked amazement, others sat picking the tiny glass shards of screen and cathode ray tube out of their hair. Nobody saw the culprit and his companions slip silently out of the bar amid the state of turmoil.

Now outside, Aden and Agent Orange were laughing uncontrollably in their drunkenness, before Aden began goading the ghost. 'Are you awake now, you comatose bastard? Television is the drug of the nation. Ninety nine per cent of the planet is hooked up to a fucking machine. My mother's so fucking interested in the lives of these two dimensional people that she's lost interest in her own. My da's the same; they can only communicate to each other through the damned TV set. Ye know, did shithead leave fuckwit, did that bastard recover from his freak tractor accident!'

'It's a government conspiracy designed to manipulate the public consciousness, duping the populace into believing it's only capable of going to work, having kids and retiring at sixty. It's sucking the real life out of you, man,' continued

Saul to the ghost, who was starting to freak out inside. The three stood around him awaiting his response, which wasn't going to arrive.

Orange broke the uneasy silence. 'The only way we can have a real far from vegetable like existence is to go voluntarily insane. Once you're free in your mind you're in a heaven. We can do whatever we want.'

'Definitely,' agreed Aden, with the pure enthusiasm of a child. 'Screw this life, I'm not going home; let's travel man.'

Orange, who'd already travelled extensively, smiled in agreement. 'Coming?' he asked the other two.

'I'm a god here,' yowled Saul. 'I've no need to go anywhere.' Without uttering another word he turned and strode up the hill towards the city centre. As he reached the horizon he grew tall in the night shadows as the grey granite buildings that stretched upward around him.

The ghost, feeling suddenly exposed, wanted desperately to go back to sleep. He made his excuses and disappeared. Orange and Aden, excited at the prospect of tomorrow, headed downhill, discussing their futures in depth.

3

The three candles burnt dimly below a crudely carved African wood sculpture that stared spookily out of the wall towards Janine who sat at the other side of the tiny room, smoking a joint whilst contemplating its primitive beauty. As recently as one hundred years back, African tribespeople had worn such images on their faces into battle. Now moderns were hanging them from their walls to freak themselves out. She gave the image a mock grimace before leaning across the snoring heap of beard and dreadlocks who lay peaceful and comatose beside her to stub out her blim in another ethnic handicraft. Her sleeping companion's room was littered with such artefacts, bought on a recent trip to Kenya – or was it Tasmania? 'Pez' had spent much of the night recounting tails of his excursions, and plans to flood the country with native handicrafts, in an attempt to return civilised society to its tribal roots. Janine's own interest in Pez-the-man did not extend too far beyond the fact that he possessed a room and a bed, but she had become quite dazzled by his tales of far away places where total strangers would come and talk to you in the street, and children would hug you for no reason.

Her mother held the belief that anyone with senses could see the world in a grain of sand, so any desire to leave the borders of your own country was a superfluous frivolity. 'Let the world come to you,' she would say, before jacking up. But as we all know, it's every child's duty to rebel against their parents. In Janine's case she'd adopted a form of inverted rebellion, refusing to inject heroin on her fifteenth birthday, much to her mother's disgust, deciding instead to only partake in recreational drugs, and even dreaming of travel. The mother/daughter conflict came to a head one autumn afternoon when Janine brought a boyfriend home. The seemingly innocent youth smoked a chillum with her mother before freaking out, hightailing out of their flat, a Jefferson Airplane record under one arm, a record player under the other and an eighth of speed in between his teeth. The bizarre incident drew Janine's mother to the conclusion that children were negative assets, obstacles in nihilistic pursuit of oblivion.

Showing her only daughter to the door of their squat she said, 'Don't worry about it babe. You're well tuned in now. It's time to drop out on your own. Kill 'em off, Janie.'

Janine looked into her mother's soulless brown eyes, gave her a confused frown and walked out the door, never looking back.

Living off her wits proved not to be to much of a problem. It was the nineteen nineties and sex was religion, sitting at the core of popular consciousness. Most blokes would do just about anything for a shag. She couldn't understand why the majority of her friends had only one boyfriend when there were so many to choose from. She found having sex with the same person for more than a fortnight just plain boring. Sex was exercise, even a good time, nothing more. Certainly not some holy religious sacrament. It was also a great way to get in some serious browsing time in their bedrooms she thought, grabbing a handful of brightly coloured pendants and carvings of deities with big penises, and shoving them into her tie dyed bag. Sitting down on the edge of Pez's DIY futon, she laced up her silver Doc Martens. The yellow sun had just begun to seep through the worn sheet nailed to the cracked front window; definitely a good time to leave.

Planting a kiss on Pez's tattooed left temple, she whispered, 'Equal distribution of assets, gorgeous. What's mine is yours.'

Then she padded silently through the half open door and out into the sunshine. It was one of those gloriously paradoxical mornings when the sky hung without a cloud and the sun shone so brightly that every reflective surface gleamed like a new star, but gave off no heat, so the cold cut through you like a laser. Janine shuddered, pulling her thick woollen llama fudgepacker jacket tightly around herself. After placing a pair of wraparound green shades over her eyes, she headed up the street into the rising sun.

Pez's room sat on top of a kebab shop on a main road, near to the edge of the city. It was still dawn and the street relatively deserted – save for a few pensioners who'd braved the cold weather to catch the early bargains down at their local supermarket. They did not know quite what to make of the brightly clad shaded young woman walking towards them. Time was moving so fast for them these days that they didn't really know how to keep up any more, and the confusion seemed to emanate from these new people who were appearing in greater numbers every day.

Janine peered over her green glasses, blue eyes gleaming in the sunlight, and grinned as she passed the two confused looking geriatrics. This had to be the best part of the day for her, hardly anyone around and very little chance of street sadness. 'Excellent!' she thought.

'You fucking bitch!' She turned around to see a fuming Pez, his previously amiable face contorted into a twisted mask of hatred, come galloping towards her, dreadlocks flying in the wind like some screaming bearded medusa.

'Jesus Christ!' uttered Janine to herself, blind fear whisking her across the road, and down an alleyway towards the park.

4

Aden watched three gulls soar into the horizon and proceeded to roll over on to his stomach, hands cupped under his thickly stubbled chin. He became quickly enthralled by the glistening dew droplets which hung from the green grass blades and clovers below him. As he looked further he saw each droplet subdivided into more droplets, each created with its own unique design. 'Worlds within worlds,' he wondered, feeling a bit frightened all of a sudden, tripping out and loving it.

Looking over his left shoulder he saw an excited Agent Orange waving him over, a clump of small indiscernible objects clutched between his soiled fingers. Aden jumped up and ran over to see his friend's discovery as if possessed by the devil, eager to discover the source of all the excitement.

'Magic mushrooms, hundreds of them!' cried Orange.

'They look just like tiny brown nipples,' replied Aden, with equal enthusiasm.

'Shit, they do don't they. And they go blue when you squeeze them, watch.'

Aden did so intensely, as Orange pressed a small mushroom cap between his thumb and forefinger and producing a flow of pale blue liquid, which ran down the ridge of his arm on to his red coat-sleeve.

The pair began scouring the grass around a gnarled old oak tree, stuffing the crop into plastic bags. So wrapped up in their harvest were the two travellers that they failed to notice a breathless Janine come hurtling towards them, still clutching her bag but without her shades, which had been lost in the chase. Her pursuer, the panting Pez, was in hot pursuit and gaining ground, spewing phlegm and spit amid gasps and curses.

As she approached, Orange caught sight of her in the corner of his eye, taking the image first as an hallucination, but then angered as he realised she was destroying a perfectly healthy crop of mushrooms. He turned to protest, but was cut off in mid-sentence as Janine grabbed him by the shoulders, looked deep into his spaced out green eyes and said in between gasps, 'He... He wants to rape me. Please help!' before speeding off. By now, Pez was almost on top of them. Without any hesitation, Orange ran over to the oak tree and, picking up his didgeridoo, swung the instrument into Pez's knees as he flew through. Pez crumpled on to the wet grass into a pain wracked heap, his face locked into a grimace of pain and frustration which continued as Orange began to lay into him. Aden ran over to join in.

'Who is he?' he asked between punches.

'Some fucking rapist,' replied Orange. He stopped his beating and wiped the sweat from his brow, then proceeded to remove the unfortunate's clothing. 'I mean it. I mean, it's the least we can do. Physical punishment's nothing to these guys. What he needs is a good dose of public humiliation, that should at least keep him off the streets for a while, ye know what I'm saying?' he continued, whilst pulling off one of Pez's paraboots and throwing it idly over a hedge and into a duck pond on the other side, where it quickly sank into the murky waters.

'I agree irrefutably,' replied Aden grimly, pulling a bowie knife from his jacket. 'And these dreads are certainly not for you, ye sick bastard.' Aden prodded Pez, who could do nothing but groan and began slicing off the thick mats of hair, placing each lock on to a neat pile beside the victim's head, putting one in a pocket as a trophy.

Orange gazed far into the distance and noticed a black-clad figure on a bike, cycling in their direction. Obviously a policeman. Leaving Pez to his remaining garments he gripped Aden by the shoulder.

Wide-eyed and slightly afraid he said, 'Let's skin out of here, I think it's the police.'

Aden jumped up and quickly followed Orange through a parting in the hedge, leaving Pez to wallow shoeless in misfortune.

The fancy dressed witch cycled by, holding her tall witch's hat steady with one hand as she peered over at the figure on the grass, not stopping to investigate.

5

'How many did you pick?' asked Corral, a thirty something single, but solvent, mother of one. She peered down into the steaming bubbling saucepan on her stove, whilst tightening the cord of her starry dressing gown.

'Well over three hundred,' replied Orange, picking through the soggy mass. 'We'd have gotten more, but something ran into us.'

'Three hundred's fine. Definitely enough for a party. The whole crowd's gonna be loaded.'

Corral looked through the kitchen serving hatch into her purple red schemed living room, where Aden lay flat on his back. He stared at the fumes of his joint as they caught in the light of the window, enjoying his trance. He and Orange had arrived, spaced out and unannounced, three days previously, much to the delight of her little son and to the mixture of apprehension and delight of herself. Delight at having some interesting company again and an untechnological source of entertainment for Lucio and apprehension due to the unfailing fact that Orange would inevitably bring an element of chaos with him. She was still trying to work out how he'd convinced her to throw a party, but hell, it was Halloween, she thought, throwing the remaining mushrooms into her pots, it'd be positive.

She felt a light prod on the back of her left thigh, and turned to see a green-faced dwarf playfully jabbing her with a plastic trident. The young mischief maker then proceeded to dance around the kitchen, waving his weapon in the air.

'Look mum, I'm the devil,' cried Lucio.

'Oh you are, are you?' she replied. 'Well, why don't you go and play with your friends next door.'

Lucio bounded through the kitchen door, pole-vaulting over the spreadeagled Aden and into the open arms of Orange, who sat lounging in an easy chair. They began pulling faces and throwing dried spaghetti at Aden, who was as yet too stoned to respond.

The sun had set four hours before, and people were streaming into Corral's house by the dozen. Dracula, Sid Vicious and Frankenstein's daughter had all turned up to join the fun. Corral's mushroom tea had been and gone, and those who had missed out had begun to trip off the vibes of those who had. Spooky psychedelic sounds were ripping through the air, as Aden half walked, half staggered through into the kitchen. He'd taken more than enough mushroom tea and spirit, and now believed himself to be the Prince of Darkness. He adjusted his plastic fangs and cruised towards his next victim. Gliding past a couple enjoying a good long kiss, he stared in amazement as their faces merged, and then stretched apart again like mozzarella. Another face expanded to twice its normal size, before disappearing through the doorway. It was like being in Star Trek. Maybe it was Star Trek, he thought, a slight panic creeping up on him. But it was too early in the evening to mongue out in a corner somewhere; he had to find blood.

Janine stood gazing out of the kitchen window down on to the street below. That morning's episode had given her a serious attack of paranoia. Pez wasn't the first bloke she'd stung in the but he'd been the first one to find out about it whilst he'd been within earshot. She could see dozens of angry men conspiring against her, all planning to hunt her down and then really fuck her up. The net was definitely closing in on her and she wanted out, as quickly as possible; but how?

She felt a jolt and someone planted a hickey on her white neck. Turning around sharply she grabbed the assailant by the shoulders, and planted her knee in between his legs, sending him crumpling to the floor. Aden looked up, a confused frown appearing on his pale face.

'But why?' he groaned. 'You were my mission.'

Janine was still angry, but was beginning to realise that she may have overreacted slightly, so she half-heartedly consoled him. 'Look mate, I didn't mean to hurt you so hard, but I'm a bit on the edge at the moment, you know what I mean? I'm sorry if you're in any pain, but I think it might be better if you just fuck off and leave me alone.'

'It's you, isn't it? The damsel in distress?' called Orange, totally unaware of the earlier incident and the passed out party goer he'd just stepped on as he made his way over, recognising Janine, and more than willing to reap any rewards that might be on offer for his dashing heroics.

'Oh yeah, right. I remember now, the two guys in the park.' She looked down at Aden and ran her fingers through his hair, kissing him on the forehead. 'Look mate, I'm really sorry about that. I had no idea who you were. I was in some real shit you know. It's lucky you've found me. What happened to Pez anyway? I think maybe he'll creep up on me. Everyone that walks down the street looks like him, for some reason.'

Orange laughed, 'Pez was it. He's not going anywhere, trust me. I'm Secret Agent Orange by the way, and this is my sorcerer's apprentice, Aden.

Aden, who'd by now recovered, was sitting cross legged and rolling a spliff, looked up and grinned. Janine smiled back and they sat together in a tight circle reliving the day's events, and pursuing a mañana conversation, sensing that their lines were running together. Soon becoming oblivious to the hallucinations surrounding them and eager to formulate a master plan to leave the island and invade Europe.

6

'So it's settled then,' said Orange. 'We wait until that big supermarket down the high street is really heaving this afternoon, and raid as much food as we can handle. We then hitch down to Dover, which we should reach by tomorrow morning, and take a ferry to France.

'France, that's like Paris, isn't it?' smiled Aden. 'Paris, shit... And there's three of us. That's a triangle, super strong, full of energy, unstoppable.'

The three had talked the sun up and showed no signs of tiring. Janine had put on a recently acquired pair of blue metallic shades, to shade herself from the piercing morning sun, letting her eyes take in the aftermath of the previous night's revelry. Plastic cups were strewn all over the place and butts of all kinds stuck out of plant pots, nostrils and earholes of dead and out of it party guests who were strewn as evenly as the fallen streamers and discarded Halloween costumes. The scene was pretty normal, far from startling in Janine's world. She was more satisfied with the fact that she'd become part of a clan, and a moving one at that. It had been easy getting enthralled in Orange's crazy theories and ideas about their place in the universe. She quite liked the idea of being a free radical floating in space; so much so in fact, that she might fancy it if they all slept together. Her future was with them, and any presupposed duty or principle attached to her past life was by now firmly out the window.

'I'm hungry. Let's eat,' she cried.

7

Shoppers of all shapes and sizes scooted in and around the Food Friends supermarket precinct, looking for the night's meal and looking for a bargain. The three travellers, having waved Corral and her party goodbye, were now scouting around without a cent to their name. Orange grabbed a vacant trolley, pausing briefly as he wondered what to do with it.

'Have you done this before?' he asked Janine, who was in the process of waking up from her daze and Aden who was only too happy to remain in his as he watched the queues of shoppers scream by like manic clockwork toys, crashing into each other and cursing their way towards the fruit section.

'No, never. But I'll try anything once. These people are more in outer space than I am; it'll be a breeze,' answered Aden.

'Only when my dinner depended on it,' replied Janine, smiling at the zebra who trotted by.

'Yeah, it's gonna be no problem. Just watch out for those store detectives. Someone told me they're everywhere,' smiled Orange, as he pushed the gleaming aluminium cart through the entrance, followed by Janine and Aden, who smiled at everyone who could see them.

'There's so much choice,' said Aden, picking up a bunch of black grapes, and carefully sampling several before putting them carefully into the trolley. 'It's a fruitarian's dream, and a carnivore's nightmare. Let's get some bananas.'

The aisles, filled with rows of foods of all kinds, from all over the world, and all packaged temptingly, seemed endless. Janine sat down on the edge of the potato counter and listened to a couple arguing over a cucumber, the last one on the shelf. The two, who'd presumably never met before, were tugging at the long green vegetable as if their dinner parties depended on it.

'I saw it first. A person just can't move in on another's find like that. If you don't let go I'll call the manager,' said one.

The other, a hard-faced woman of about fifty, tightened her grip, to the extent that her end of the bargain was crushed to mush in her hand. At that instant, an assistant hauled a cage full of lush green cucumbers into view.

'Fuck this, I need some cheese,' Janine thought, unimpressed by the performance. She glided round into aisle five where Aden was now examining the herb racks with great interest, discussing the pros and cons of each one with an elegant blonde who smiled in distaste at his rugged demeanour. Aden, noticing her lack of interest, pulled a face before grabbing as many of the herbs and spices as he could carry in one go and dumped them in the trolley as Orange sped by.

'What's her problem?' Orange asked.

'Her world is dominated by style and size,' Aden answered, somewhat disappointedly.

By now the trolley was filling fast with more goods than you could possibly imagine, so much so that many of the items were suddenly uncontainable within the confines of the metal cart and had begun to fall out leaving a trail of consumables behind them. Janine had no desire to stop and pick them up, but had become quite unnerved by a seedy looking stubbly pensioner who had been sticking close since aisle three. She mentioned her fear to Orange who turned to catch the man looking at them and quickly turned his attention to a box of cake mix as he realised he'd been spotted.

'He could be a store detective,' whispered Orange. 'Apparently they disguise themselves as flashers so no one will notice them. It's all right, though, we can lose him in toothpastes and cosmetics.'

Janine stared back, biting her cheek, and then giggled.

Under instruction, Aden, who was now pushing the laden vehicle, took the next corner fast, sending several packets of peanuts flying through the air into another trolley. With an instinct that surprised him he deftly wove between two trolleys and a screaming child skipping aisles eight and nine before heading into aisle ten.

'Phew, I think we've lost him,' mused Janine looking back. 'Let's get out of here, this factory's got no tune to it.'

Orange and Aden agreed wholeheartedly and they joined a checkout queue.

The queue winded back into the aisle like an overstuffed python. Mums stuffed piles of unpurchased goods into the mouths of their children to keep them happy, and to their fellow consumers vented their anger at the time they had to waste and the increasing price of fish fingers. Aden had pushed the trolley to the end of one such queue and lit a cigarette, blowing the nicotine fumes into the ceiling miles above. The couple in front, both in the autumn of their lives, were giving him disapproving glances and muttering to each other about the shame of it all. Not so much the shame of this dazed young man smoking in a non-smoking area but at the state of his trolley which was now spilling over and under. The lad's inexperience had led him to place the soft goods at the bottom, a fatal error that allowed the heavy goods on top to crush them. Banana and grape mush began to ooze through the grating and on to the floor tiling below.

Time slowed as the trolley and its passengers crawled through to their final destination and freedom. Orange, exhausted from lack of sleep, was allowing himself to become hypnotised by the bland supermarket melodies piped all around him. Janine had begun to worry how he was going to pull off his plan. The checkout girl was looming larger and larger in front of them, looking strangely at her new customers as they edged closer, while scanning each item through a bleeping laser bar code reading device.

Customers paid and went. Money and plastic changed hands and till receipts buzzed and spewed out of the machinery until finally Orange, Janine, Aden and their food reached the beginning of the queue and the end of the line, the trolley, now empty, was pushed to the other side, and the piles of food were slowly moving along the black rubber conveyer and neatly packed into bags at the end of the till by Sil the checkout girl, who smiled coyly at Aden as he tried to chat her up. The damage, astronomical even by Food Friends standards, was settled by Orange who whipped a gold card from his inside pocket. The formalities were dealt with, the trolley was loaded and Aden stole a kiss from Sil before the three flew back outside, freewheeling the trolley out of the car park through a puddle and into an underpass.

'What are we gonna do with all this shit?' asked Janine, munching on a hefty slice of dark yellow cheese.

Orange pondered this for a moment, then wheeled the trolley up to a traveller who sat cross legged under the bridge, waiting for change. 'Lucky day my friend,' he said leaving the trolley by the man's side with the forged gold card on top before following Aden out of the underpass.

Broken clouds passed overhead. 'What did you get?' he asked Janine, looking back over his shoulder.

'Just some cheese, and mushrooms,' she replied in between chewing.

Aden looked around and grinned, taking a swig from his stealthily concealed bottle of rum. 'Have some rum. It's what the sailors drink. How do we get to Dover?'

8

Janine remembering an old film she'd once seen where two hitchhikers struggling to get a lift hid in some bushes whilst the third, a young woman, stood, seemingly alone, on the roadside and stuck her thumb out, increasing her friends' chances of a lift. Putting the cultural theory into practice, she took down her hair and stood in the lay-by of an A-road like a lorry driver's fantasy – eyes sparkling and hair blowing wildly in the gale. Unsurprisingly, it was no time before an articulated truck driving through pulled to a halt struck by the image. Janine smiled wryly and jumped up on the footplate to get in with the driver whose gold teeth shone back, only too happy to let her into his fantasy. His golden grin, however, quickly lost its lustre as Aden and Orange sprang out of the bushes and into the cab with them.

'I'm Janine and these are my two friends. They're travelling to Dover like me and you. Do you like cheese?'

The truck driver was by now slightly embarrassed that he'd been caught in a drift, especially with the seedy erotic gallery of nude women hanging droopily around him.

'You see that photo there – no, left a bit – next to the girl covered in potato peelings – yeah, that's the one.' Janine pointed out a healthy breasted girl holding a riding crop and leather saddle.

'So. What's the mystery, darling?' replied the driver, with a smirk.

'She was my little sister. I didn't really know her but she's dead now, some incurable disease, I think,' said Janine, lying through her teeth but always on the case against pornography and more than happy to put a burn on the man's joy department.

'Oh really? Your sister? I'm sorry.' The driver looked at his passenger curiously and then tore the magazine cutting from the wall of the cab and out of the open window. 'Happy now?'

'No, not really. What do you get off on looking at such cheap tat, you fucking arsehole? Christ knows what you'd have done if I'd been travelling on my own. I've a good mind to report you to the police. The vice squad would sort you out no problem. Sex offenders don't get a good time of it inside, know what I mean?' replied Janine, not quite sure what she was talking about but getting into her stream of consciousness, unashamed that the driver was now feeling fairly uncomfortable, his concentration gone to pot. Aden, who'd fallen asleep, like Orange, as soon as they'd got in the cab, had now awoken, surprised to hear Janine goading their chauffeur in such a manner. He propped his eyes open, trying hard not to fall back asleep, more interested in whether or not Janine's opinions might get them chucked out in the middle of nowhere.

'Hi, my name's Jim,' he interjected. 'Your truck is the fucking business. My uncle is in the same business; he's a techno nomad like yourself. Where did you get this tiger fur upholstery?'

Janine glared at her companion, furious at his unnecessary interruption. 'Techno nomad – what's your trip, Jim? His name's Barry and he's a borderline paedophile. Have you seen this crap?' she continued, pointing to the remaining pictures.

Barry, growing increasingly confused, had begun to sweat profusely, his unhealthy odour starting to reek a smell straight from hell not dissimilar to rotting vegetables, opening his window but closing it immediately as the torrential rain from outside began to pour in. The stench remained. Janine and Aden looked at each other not knowing whether to laugh or hold their noses. The grim vapour drifted silently inside the cab making it seem very small. As the cooling fan spread it evenly the tiny particles soon reached the heaving nostrils of Agent Orange who awoke with a start.

'Jesus Christ,' he coughed, then adjusted his thinking, having realised the origin of his discomfort. 'Hi, there, I'm Barry – no I'm not, that's you – shit, I'm Orange.'

Barry laughed, unable to hear the words clearly over the roar of the engine. 'You're an orange, *yeah man*, I'm a melon.'

Everyone laughed, all for different reasons. The atmosphere, though still unpleasantly potent, had relaxed considerably since Janine's outburst and the four travellers mellowed out, taking in the view which, seen through the rainswept windscreen of the truck, was not unlike an impressionist painting. Orange peered through the watery haze at the blurry trees and houses as they sped by, Janine and Aden put imaginary bets on the raindrops, guessing which ones would reach the bottom of the windscreen first, while Barry relaxed, not happy, or unhappy, just grateful that he would soon be able to return to his own head space.

9

The big lorry bounced across the rain soaked tarmac of the
Dover dockyards and into a free space. Barry looked at his
passengers and smiled smugly.

'That's all folks. I'm off to sleep for a while. I'm sorry to
say it, but this is goodbye. There should be a ferry to where
you want to go – let me think – tomorrow morning. See ya
later, kids,' he said pointing Orange towards the passenger
door which promptly opened out on to the damp trailer
park.

'Sure you won't come with us?' grinned Aden looking
back as he slammed the door shut. He was quite relieved to
be out in the open and the relatively fresh air, and took in
the view for a moment before being struck by a new notion.

'How am I going to get to France if I haven't got a pass-
port?' he asked Orange, not hiding the puzzled expression
on his face.

Janine looked surprised at his confusion but then
clasped her hands over her mouth, realising she was in the
same situation.

Orange beamed. 'Don't worry about such trivialities, my
friends,' he said jovially. 'There's a secret way through the
world which nobody knows about. An old yogi told me
about it.'

He turned and began walking out of the park, away from
the ferry terminals and into a fog bank, followed by Aden
and Janine who were discussing whether their friend was

just taking the piss or whether his marbles had just come unstuck along the way. The tarmac gave way to a thin winding gravel path shadowed on both sides by lush green grass. Magic mushrooms poked through the blades in abundance but went unnoticed by the dreadlocked sorcerer as he strode past, dipping his head as the path began to slope upwards towards the famed white cliffs of Dover. Janine had begun to feel a tad manic depressive, but did not want to express her pessimisms to Aden who was wondering why his friend kept looking up into the sky towards the setting sun. They reached the top of the cliff and Orange sat down on the damp grass, looking towards the sea which was shrouded by fog through which the sun still burned.

Janine sat down, and sighed as Aden began skinning a joint. 'Is this yoga then?' she asked in mock excitement. 'If we om out here for five years maybe we'll be able to levitate across.'

Orange frowned but refused to be put off by her sarcasm. 'Please, you should be happy. This is a real special day. All the ingredients are here for a safe painless flight. A yellow sun is shining at four o'clock through dense south sea mist.' He paused and then produced a brightly woven pocket-sized sack from inside his coat which he opened, producing three tiny triangles which he passed around. Aden looked at the small object, realising it was a window pane – a rare hallucinogen named after its transparent appearance. The effects, apparently, are best discovered by putting the flat pane under your eyelid. But he still wondered how such an innocent looking device could possibly get them to France.

'My mother used to take these,' said Janine. 'She always got excited when they came around; she'd lock herself in her room for days experimenting with them. But how's this going to get us to France?'

Orange showed them how to place the gear under their eyelids after asking them to sit in a triangle at the cliff's edge with himself and Aden at the base and Janine at the apex looking out across the Channel. 'Don't be afraid – it's easy. Just close your eyes. Don't think of England, Aden, picture the Place du Tertre artists painting portraits of cool Parisienne ladies drinking coffee in the early hours... Janine, imagine endless avenues of poplar trees... Vaya con Dios,' he said as the wind caressed them.

Orange himself didn't quite know what to visualise, but he held tight on to his fear as the gleaming white image of an outstretched claw shot out of the darkness, grabbing him and his three friends and carrying them away. He screwed up his eyes, desperately wanting to wake up. Just a few more moments. He felt like he'd been dragged to the bottom of the ocean, the extreme pressure crushing his spirit until he could breathe no longer. Unseen forces were attacking him from all sides; another moment and he'd be there, but his dream could not understand time. Feeling a kind of rigor mortis set in he could contain himself no longer and howled.

10

Aden and Janine, lost in their picture thoughts, awoke with a start as Orange's primal scream whistled through the air. He turned towards them, his face white, sweating profusely. Orange wasn't feeling to good, but managed to hide this from his two companions who were by now quite startled at their new location – a rain glistened Paris pavement some four kilometres from the Arc de Triomphe and just around the corner from the infamous Moulin Rouge. Their rapid location transfer had changed Aden's thick black hair to blond and Janine's fingernails from blue to bright green, but she had now become more concerned with the thousand year old man who had begun to pinch at her coat sleeve and jabber away in a grizzly foreign tongue.

'Je suis désolé, mademoiselle. Vous êtes fatiguée, n'est-ce pas? Donnez-moi une cigarette muh huh, huh.'

Janine, whose knowledge of this language was extremely poor, poked the man in the eye. 'No monsieur, I have no cigarette to give you – I smoked them all on the way, but I have a stick of gum if you fancy altering the mood of your breath.'

Deeply unhappy with the offer, the man growled before scuttling away down a side street towards the Moulin Rouge.

Janine shared her annoyance with Aden who had only just managed to come to terms with his situation and had begun scouting the area looking for girls. The ones he'd seen in Toulouse-Lautrec paintings in magazines and art galleries long ago, those he saw here were dressed to kill, looking at his face with a mild hunger but ultimately being unimpressed by his unaspiring demeanour. Quite scared he looked round at Janine who just shrugged and held his hand, taking a long confused drag from her cigarette as Orange took the didgeridoo from his rucksack, lotused and ommed out.

'Let's go shopping,' she said excitedly.

Aden shrugged and gave her a cool kiss that spun her along as the urban sounds and images flew past towards oblivion. Leaving his friend a long glance he moved away into his future.

The long avenue in front of them was unexpectedly seedy but not depressing; the shop windows sold pornographic posters finely presented in glass settings that aimed to entice you in. In a decidedly reactionary mood Janine picked up a rolling stone and catapulted it through one of the cases much to the dismay of the proprietor who chased after them, prevented from doing so only by his age and weight. The crowd was too heavy and his targets just blended in.

'I thought I was wild,' marvelled Aden. 'I'm thirsty – let's have a beer.

Well away from the incident, they sat at an iron table chained to the floor as an angry man poured them a beer and a spirit. The passing crowd was in no hurry to stop. A Toulouse-Lautrec painting it was not, but it was still full of colour. A taxi pulled in to the kerb, containing seven men and two brightly painted women arguing intensely over the price of the fare. Half the struggle was getting out; once this had been achieved, the taller of the five travellers swore at the female driver, ripping a wad of blue and red notes from his crocodile wallet which he threw into the air as the driver laughed, catching the falling paper as it floated gently to the earth. Janine caught a stray one and studied the monochrome painting on the front – a row of tall terraced mansions set behind a tidy pavement lined with tiny yearlings. 'Looks cool, shall we go?' she said dreamily, rubbing herself up against Aden's face and biting his ear as she rolled the note in between her fingers and tucked it behind his other ear.

11

Lost but unruffled, Janine and Aden led each other through the glowing avenues of their Parisienne sunset. The street population had thinned and they'd run out of things to talk about. A place to stay was first on the list and Janine decided to stop and talk to a bohemian-looking couple who'd obviously just returned from a hard day's arting about.

'*Bonsoir, mes amis. Nous sommes* aliens from another planet touring around for an expanding cultural and social experience. If you invite us in we'd be more than happy to share it with you,' asked Janine in her own unique brand of Esperanto.

The woman, tall and sweet and always open to new-comers, whispered approvingly to her companion who was too merry for an argument and gleefully shouted, '*Bienvenue*,' ushering them up the long flight of worn steps that led towards a four-storey post-revolution apartment block not unlike the one on the floating banknote. An iron concertinaed doorway opened into a red streaked marbled floorway.

'*Comment vous appelez-vous?*' asked the woman, Colletta.

'*Gorky et Maxime*,' replied the former Aden who surprised himself with his lightning ability to understand this new tongue and change his name at will.

'Well, my friends, we do not have much to offer you, but we love travelling and haven't been anywhere for a long time, so we would be grateful if you could donnez us some fabulous information of where we could stay in peaceful tranquillity under palm trees. We have a great interest in a new progressive headspace,' Colletta's companion said, who, unlike her, was barely five feet tall but possessed a face of unique wisdom and knowledge, his skin heavily lined but very well defined.

Maxime watched intently as a glistening bead of perspiration trickled down a crevice in his forehead that caught it affectionately before it rolled down his curved nose on to the floor. She took his arm as they walked through the apartment door and began conversing with him about tales of far away places and magical cultures.

The high-ceilinged apartment was distinctly minimalist in style. The windows were shuttered by dark venetian blinds so that very little natural light could pierce the rooms which contained no pictures or photographic images, just chequered walls and two large television sets which had been left on throughout the day and were buzzing with random activity. Maxime and Pieter slumped down on a futon leaving Colletta and Gorky to rustle some food up in the kitchen. The latter perched on the table watching whilst Colletta gracefully danced around the kitchen, peeling vegetables with her long fingernails before slicing them and frying them in a wok with all manner of spices and herbs.

'I tend not to eat meat, you know,' she said. 'All life that moves long distances is sacred to me – eating flesh and blood from another being has an uncalming effect on people one could say, my relations were in the meat trade. I don't know it's horrible imagery, like a vampire movie.' She widened her eyes as Gorky looked on.

'I've never really seen it in that way before,' he said. 'Surely if something's already dead then there's no harm in eating it.'

Colletta ignored his comment and proceeded to tap in time with the sizzling organics in the oily pan. Grey snakes spiralled up out of it and wafted into the next room where Pieter had become transfixed by the day's events flashing from the TV set.

A riot broke out in the Pigalle district of the city today. Stones were thrown by feminist protesters in anger at the thriving sex industry. Glass was smashed but no human fatalities occurred.

'I hate this violence,' declared Pieter, waving his hand towards the flickering screen. 'Tell me where in the world I should go. I have need of a peaceful conclusion to my life,' he continued, firing the infra red beam across the room to extinguish the commentary. His sadness at his inability to alter world events, however, was not long lived, and he grinned at his guest who had begun to bite her lip nervously. 'I have never seen the mountains, white peaks soaring into the sky, narrow ravines and red-cloaked children playing in gushing mountain streams. I could live with that, no worries. The trouble is, I never know whether these places exist now or in the past or just in my imagination.'

'All these places exist; you just have to believe and you'll find them,' pretensed Pieter, stretching out across the room and encircling Maxime in his surprisingly long arms. She refused to put up any resistance to her strange host and enjoyed the warm physical contact as they awaited their meal which sailed in on the arms of Gorky whose face, flushed by the steaming kitchen, was more than glad to return to the cool breeze provided by the humming air-conditioning unit in the corner.

'Where's this recipe from? It tastes fantastic,' munched Maxime.

'I made it up. You could say it's from everywhere. It may inspire us to leave, I think. We have been ghosts in this city for too long. Pieter has had the urge for some time to become a phantom, flying through many countries with great speed, unnoticed but not unwelcome.'

'I have had such a desire for some time,' said Pieter. 'Do you know of any place we can go? You and your friend can stay here for as long as you like, paint it, trash it – whatever you want.

'I have an uncle living in Mirondavo,' answered Gorky, 'on a beach near a rainforest. Its location is so separate and unusual that it is the only habitat of a very wide and diverse range of species – cool, huh?'

'We will go to this place *mañana!*' boomed Pieter taking a mouthful of spicy food and savouring each flavour on his taste buds before letting the ingredients slide effortlessly into his well-kept stomach.

12

After two days Pieter and Colletta had left for Mirondavo, accompanied by a few possessions and the address of Gorky's relative, leaving Gorky and Maxime to enjoy the simple comforts of the home Gorky, won over by Colletta's concept of zen living, frequented the local markets returning with colourful armfuls of strangely shaped organics, lovingly preparing them for Maxime who had set about redecorating, the chequered walls now replaced by spectral stripes which lined the walls like tangible energy.

The two nomads had also begun to frequent a local coffee bar named *Real Fantasy*, a local haunt for anyone interested in sitting there outside, watching the world float by.

Maxime began talking with a travelling DJ. 'My feeling tells me you are new here too. I myself am waiting for my decks to arrive – have you seen them?' he asked, lazily sipping his black coffee through a green straw as he described the equipment and its shiny steel packaging with a series of sweeping hand movements.

'What are you mixing?' she asked playfully.

'It's a combination of hypnotic trance and uplifting house music for your ears. It's my only art.'

'When you arrive you must come and play for us. We are four storeys high and don't get any visitors,' replied Maxime, waiting for Gorky to join in.

'Yes, yes, come any time,' said Gorky, 'we have no music inside and I've sold the TV. Do you have anywhere to stay?'

'A place to stay, you are too kind, my friend. I would not have it any other way,' assented the DJ easing a long stick of tobacco from behind his ear and lighting it on a false finger that had been craftily adapted into a lighter holder. 'I lost this in a machine accident,' he continued. 'A coiling mechanism. I was half asleep from many hours of work and the fucker ripped it right out of its socket. Saves me rooting around in my pockets, though. I love this city. It's more dead than alive, but dead in a uniquely vibrant way. The women are open-minded to a very agreeable extent and very aggressive between the sheets, you know what I'm talking about. Like tigresses. My back's covered in scratches; I have to lie on my front, it hurts so much.'

The DJ, whose name still escaped them, fuelled their night with tales of lost records, angry husbands and brushes with the underworld as if he was a burning oil well, each story interlocking without a hitch, his cigarettes glowing all the time in the dark. Encouraged to come and stay, the man accompanied his new friends back inside, zapped by light beams that shot across the sky.

'Batman, we don't need you,' he cried, dancing along the sidewalk to an unreal rhythm that piloted his stocky body.

'I like it,' smiled Maxime, tugging her friend's jacket, bringing him closer into her happy presence.

13

A well-travelled herring gull recently returned from a season on the dumps circled the St Denis area of Paris in search of a better class of meal. The food on the refuse tip near Compiègne, though abundant, was of a curious origin and the hungry gull was now frighteningly susceptible to hallucinations, snapping his beak at any passing object either imaginary or material.

Many metres below him, the bird spied a series of coloured crotchets and quavers floating out of one of the many apartment block windows. Although the gull could hear no sound as yet, he was fascinated by the notes as they coiled in an undisciplined circular motion not unlike a rainbow whirlpool in the sky. Eager to discover the source, the big bird swooped down to investigate, landing on the ledge of the open window of Gorky's flat.

Peering in through the blinds, it watched mesmerised by the music as it flew out of the spinning turntable tracing the coloured lines of energy before soaring out of the cracks in the blind. The gull snapped away, frustrated that his efforts had left him without a meal.

Inside, Gorky and Maxime listened, smoked and drank as they'd been doing for most of the week as DJ Halonn spun his endless collection, masterfully blending the elements together creating an eternal flow of wall to sky sound. Halonn's mixing had brought with it visitations from the local residents' association, who, after sampling a

tray of Gorky's concoctions, decided to forget their griev-
ances, shut the fuck up and chill out as the music-induced
hypnosis continued. All their visitors stopped their con-
sumer lifestyle and took days off work for no reason, talking
amongst themselves about how they should do likewise, for
the sake of cultural and social relations within the
community.

'These people are driving me insane. They talk, and
listen, say hello and shake hands, but never smile, everything is formal and regulated by social convention. Argh!
I'm sorry, but this is it. I have to leave, find pastures new,
hit the road, fuck off, skin out – you know what I say?' said
Gorky one misty morning over a cup of orange tea.

'If you feel that way, then yes, it might be better if you
hit the trail – you're one of those odd gods who's only at
home when you're not,' replied Maxime, putting on a brave
face but secretly sad at her companion's on-the-spot
decision to abandon her with Halonn and his decks. She'd
thought that maybe their trips would be wired together
through into old age, but Gorky's restlessness was something that could not be overcome by one woman. She
planted a final kiss on his cracked lips before slowly closing
the concertina door behind him, secretly watching him
through the keyhole as he disappeared down the spiral
staircase back into the normal world.

14

Gorky, though his travelling time had been relatively short, had grown fond of train stations, and especially this one. Having left his life with Maxime in search of a new one, the traveller was making the most of his brief stay in limbo, sitting knees apart in front of a pillar under a hole in the glass roof which lay high above him, the squat of generations of pigeons and ingenious rats, but Gorky's attention preferred to observe life at ground level. Although his reasons for liking the place did not extend to vibrant enthusiasm, he admired its intransigent nature. The station was always there but its insides buzzed with activity. Huge boards advertising both foods and destinations flickered and revolved in time to the turbulent music of the crowd, a stew of commuters, hustlers, live animals, flashing cleaning vehicles, flashing mac wearers, twitching drug addicts and himself. He lit a fag as one junkie walked past.

His train south was still another two hours from leaving, so Gorky swapped senses, closing his eyes and taking a fill through the ears. The music hissed like static and echoed around the interior in a kind of tubular roar, before escaping out on to the train tracks. Fragments of conversations crackled and twisted around him, decoding into a language that spoke directly to him. Gorky found it scary but on the whole a positive tune, one of fluidity and passive chaos, until the deep guttural tones of a didgeridoo filtering the uneven melody enticed Gorky to open his eyes and go and investigate the source. Pushing himself impatiently, a myriad of patterns and colour invaded his vision and killed off his balance. He spun for a second then fell to his knees into the hard marble floor.

'*Il conto!*' jeered a passing commuter, happy to see the younger man hit a patch of psychedelic shock. Gorky, whose vision had now recovered, stared after the man with a tiger's anger in his eyes, making as if to pounce in his offender's direction. The latter looked back, the criticism wiped from his face and replaced by a minor dose of fear which encouraged him to hurry along as Gorky slowly stood up and followed the dreamtime humming.

As he had hoped, the playing end of the didgeridoo was being hurred into by Orange who sat before the crowds of intransigent people. Though the player had been freewheeling the Parisian pavements for over two months now, his persona shone brighter than ever. Covered in a thinly striped multicoloured customised boiler suit, attached to which were the faces of tiny watches all ticking at different times, he raised an eyebrow as Gorky approached and stopped playing as the younger man stooped to place his remaining centimes in the battered hat that sat amidst the litter and debris left by previous visitors.

'*Merci beaucoup, mon ami,*' he whispered as Gorky, now aware that he wasn't remembered, sat down next to him replying '*De nada.*'

'*Tu joues le kazoo, mon patron,*' replied Orange retrieving a purple instrument from his jacket pocket and handing it to Gorky, who began buzzing away in abstract time to his new friend's music, spicing the air with an energetic melody.

Not a Nice Day

1

Looking far up into the rooftops of a thriving city centre, Ryan spied a laughing man spinning a hefty looking barrel around his large hairy hands whilst moving his head rhythmically from side to side as he slowly poured a tankard full of beer down into his deep, pulsating gullet. In Ryan's estimation, this was no mean feat by anyone's standards and he would have to give the bar below him his patronage. After checking his pockets for loose change he made for the doorway, jumping a rolling drunk who spun out as he strode in.

The bar, named The Jolly Point, was themed in a kind of eighteenth century nautical style; sea dog dummies adorned the panelled walls and portholes embossed the booth partitions, allowing nosy customers to eavesdrop and spy on the neighbouring ones. Purchasing a foaming pint of beer from a seawoman-costumed barmaid, Ryan sat in one such booth, took a sip and relaxed.

The only un-naval thing in the whole place was the clientele. Ryan imagined he was living a century in the past, cruising aboard an old ocean liner bound for parts unknown, and if this was real he should really be getting more acquainted with everyone else on board, but the ones he could see were firmly cliqued, as was the fashion, so he held back the social animal urge and happily continued to indulge his senses.

Scanning the view of the other passengers aboard, Ryan found The Jolly Point a soothing combobulation of internationals chatting and drinking. Snatches of conversations discussed sex, culture, travelling and obscure philosophies, though Ryan's attention was more concentrated on the two most recent arrivals, a blooming pair of olive-skinned beauties, the first with long hair, unusual clothes and a gregarious nature and the second more mysterious and silent. She gave Ryan a long look from the bar, whispering to her friend that they should breeze over; after all, they were on a ship, everyone was in it together and there were no other booths available. Ryan flushed with pride as the two travellers glided towards him and sat down opposite without asking, both retrieving strangely labelled cartons of cigarettes from their bags, igniting the ends and sending the first wisps of blue smoke up into the ceiling where it hung in a haze before dispersing across the bar. The two women gazed at Ryan briefly with smouldering dark eyes before conversing between themselves in a lyrical foreign tongue. If he wanted to go anywhere with these two handsome strangers, an interjection was needed. He knew the first was always the hardest. Taking a cool gulp for courage, he spoke.

'Hola. Where are you going?' directing his words at them both.

The more gregarious of the two spoke for them both. 'We are young like you, diablo; we don't know where we go. This place is still very new to us. We are on a karmic journey; we are artists. Why – where does your life take you? And what is your name?'

Ryan liked her direct approach: journeys were good but he preferred stories, although a traveller's tale would be even better. He rubbed his eyes as the plumes of smoke floated irritatingly towards him.

'My name? Oh right, I'm Ryan. What do I do? Nothing at present. I'm into the art of doing nothing, cruising around waiting for a sign – an aesthetician I suppose.' he answered, steepling his long fingers down the middle of his chest.

'An aesthetician?' Rosalla, the first one, briefly looked confused and then grinned as Irene, her enigmatic partner, gave her an interpretation, licking her teeth and brushing her black painted index nail down from her chin into the perspiring nape of her neck.

'*El color*, eh?' she said, analysing the bead of sweat before licking it off her hand.

Rosalla continued, 'Well, *hombre*, you look like someone who knows this place well. I don't know where you going but we'd like to travel with you for a while, show the city and we'll paint it red,' her black eyes wide open as Irene pouted in fond agreement.

Ryan, not believing his luck, ignored the deathly white angry face that peered at him through the porthole in the partition. In such company, he would gladly allow himself to be eaten alive, and in such hot weather he had to be dreaming. Downing the remainder of his pint in unison with Rosalla and Irene, they proceeded to jump ship and venture together into the outside world.

An experienced drinker frowned at Ryan as he led out, shaking his head and muttering, 'These are dangerous and strange women, Ryan, leave them now or a lonely fate awaits you.'

'Fuck. What would he know?'

The sun outside The Jolly Point, now blinding, burned the city streets making everything beautiful. Ryan moved his hands in a laid-back sweeping fashion, deciding on a left turn whilst opening the bar door politely for Rosalla and Irene, the latter brushed roughly aside by a man in bizarre androgynous clothing who unconsciously barged past and disappeared into the glare of the street to the curses that followed.

'I apologise,' said Ryan. 'Some people, there's always one to spoil the fun.'

Rosalla waved the memory away. '*De nada*. He is an imbecile. Pay it no mind.'

Now between them, Ryan gave as best he could a conducted tour of the sights surrounding them, criticising the environment as if it was his own. An inner life now embraced the idea that he was a king escorting two dark beauties around his kingdom feeling immune to the criticism from his public on the outside, jealous of his luck and actions.

'He's totally off his head,' said one.

'Arrogant arsehole,' said another.

The music of the street, usually harsh and deriding, now only added to his pleasure. Rosalla was loving it, making cutting comments of her own directed towards the unusual abundance of freakish characters roaming the streets in the steaming afternoon. Irene took Ryan's hand in hers as a seven foot tall bald man, incongruously attired in a sheepskin coat and sporting a shining steel horn through his nose, strode past carrying a small child on his shoulders which towered above the crowd, getting the best view in town. The kid waved lazily at Irene as she blew him a kiss.

'I love this town,' she said.

The pavement reached a corner, and the pedestrians waiting to cross stood in a muddled formation whilst the light stayed red. As the vehicles fumed by, the human traffic on the other side was obscured below the neck by the mechanical blur. Most heads looked blankly into the flashing light; two, however, looked straight at Ryan, Rosalla and Irene who all felt uncomfortably conspicuous. Ryan remembered the mortified white face from the porthole and could not put its recurrence down to coincidence. The face's eyes, black and sunken beneath a hooded brow, remained static as the head shook in a slow rhythm from side to side, each sweep becoming more twisted until it rotated a full one hundred and eighty degrees and moved off towards where they were heading.

'Quite freaky. I don't think I have seen anything like this before,' exclaimed Rosalla. 'It must be the weather.'

The sight soon left her mind as a man sweating beneath a long wax jacket and bent at right angles through old age and a piano lifting accident dodged the oncoming vehicles with the agility of someone younger, spewing spit and green phlegm as he went muttering and cursing to anything that dared cross his path.

The light, now green, heralded a pedestrian exodus and the crowds filed past like schools of passing fish meeting briefly in silence at a spot in the ocean before gliding away in search of food and refuge, though Irene kept looking back and marvelling at the doubled-up man, still swearing all the way.

'Come on, Irene, or we'll have to wait again,' called Rosalla over the drone of surrounding traffic. Irene heard the shout and smiled as the man wove his way around the corner, vanishing for ever, then followed her two companions north down a long tree lined avenue that extended at least two kilometres, at the end of which stood a black marbled obelisk shrouded in the cloud which was now descending to earth aggravating public perspiration and the general humidity.

'Let's go inside, Ryan,' moaned Rosalla quietly. 'It's hot out here and our hotel is just two blocks away.'

Ryan removed his shades. 'Okay,' he said.

2

Rosalla swung open the door to her room and danced through the cool conditioned air, flinging herself on the double bed while Irene watched her with half a smile out of déjà vu. Ryan, though not on home turf, retained a calm exterior despite exploding inside. If this turned out the way he wanted, he'd write his memoirs.

Irene joined Rosalla on the bed and remained in silence as she began removing her friend's clothes. Rosalla pushed herself up from her horizontal position, licked her lips, and in a flash slid her hand under Irene's top and whipped off her green lace brassiere, throwing it up into the spinning fan where it caught and whirled around, then sent a smouldering glance in Ryan's direction.

'It's so hot, diablo, what else can we do?'

Ryan grinned and looked down to unbutton his pants, but the grin broke as everything blanked out. To his confusion and utter disappointment, everything went white. Just for a second he briefly returned to the room although two tiny white rectangles hovering in front of his eyes denied him full vision. The girls had disappeared, replaced by the angry white-faced man from the pelican crossing and the bar who wore luminescent spandex, a bowler hat and a fur coat open at the neck, presumably for ventilation and to show off his obscure array of religious-looking medallions and necklaces. He stood on the bed, dancing up and down, eyes wide and shoulders hunched with thin arms stemming down to two huge hands locked into claws. The left of these held a square oblong of shiny metal encrusted with semi-precious stones, the source of Ryan's temporary blindness which was now fading, allowing him to take in the new scene before him which he soon realised was not to his liking. With his mouth open, he stared at the epicene creature before him, unimpressed by the image.

'You're that fucking downer from the bar. You shouldn't be in here – fuck off,' fumed Ryan, not taken in by the gyrations displayed before him or by the shiny flashing mirror which now waved in front of his face.

The face laughed not unlike a hyena would, its pale face tick-tocking from side to side. Suddenly it went rigid and spoke without any lip movement. 'You'd better show me some fucking respect. You are nothing here, nothing, I tell you. He laughed again. Ryan had grown irritated already as the twangy voice continued, 'Think about it Ryan. You have no money and are many miles from home. You know nobody. This planet owes you shit. The people don't speak to people they don't know and you know no one – understand?'

Ryan scoffed and reached into his pockets for his wallet to find only his hairy thighs in through the severed seams. 'Bit of a nightmare, really.'

'Yes Ryan, I am a bit of a nightmare really, but you have no choice. I am your only way home. Without me your begging it, mate, in the shit. You were never going to make it anyway. *I* know the people who make it.'

Ryan was already missing the warmth of Irene and Rosalla, especially Irene. He screwed his eyes up, wishing the intruder away, but it wouldn't work. His uncle had said travelling could be great but also hard, and that you were bound to have a few bad experiences and meet a few shits.

Maybe begging would be a better alternative to walking down the street with this wannabe ubermensch.

'If you are helping me maybe you could tell me why. We've only just met,' said Ryan.

The face scrunched into an enormous effort of thought before replying coolly in a smirk, 'I miss someone to take the piss out of.'

The unwelcome guest moved closer to Ryan, who was more annoyed and frustrated than scared and unsuccessfully tried to avoid the advance as the visitor shrouded him in his cloak like a Dracula would in the movies except without the menace.

3

The enveloping darkness opened on to a desolate neon-lit and electronically polluted street without sunlight, people or sound. The new companion, whom Ryan had decided to call Clapp, had begun to talk on an imaginary telephone, and was seemingly troubled, much to Ryan's delight. His voice, high pitched and agitated, echoed around the tall buildings which stretched into the murky green sky. Clapp stopped in mid-sentence barking a question at Ryan, 'What music you like uh?' then tapped his foot impatiently on the concrete in a camp manner whilst Ryan, surprised at the question, thought of an answer.

'Music, right, let me think. Yeah. Jungle, intelligent jungle. Do you have that where you come from?'

Clapp ignored him and continued to gabble into his imaginary phone. Surprisingly, the music of Ryan's choice began filtering through the long avenues from an unknown source at a volume which was not unpleasant. He smiled, and then beamed as Clapp disappeared down a nearby drain. 'Good riddance. What an arsehole.' Ryan peered over into the drain where Clapp had disappeared, leaving a colourful oily pool behind him which reflected a sign above, leading to the underground system.

The deep bass hid all other sound, and Ryan roamed the deserted streets trying his best not to become too confused by the hi-tech advertising media world around him and wondering what could have happened to Irene as a virtual reality topless woman danced voluptuously high above him. The feeling of having such unlimited space, and the lack of a crowd, quickly got to Ryan who lost his limited self-consciousness and began to run down the middle of the main street arms flailing in the air, spinning around until he stopped, letting the immediate world spin around him in a blur of technicoloured unnatural light. The world stopped outside an oversized picture window that protected a wall of TV screens cleverly arranged so that the picture showing on each screen alternated, creating a pleasing chequered pattern. The first, a cloudy image that flickered as violent forks of lightning split it in two and the second, an image of part of the underground system which wound its way through the city far below it, were projected on those wide-screen sets that showed you everything.

Ryan perked up as he saw Irene and Rosalla concentrating on a map which billowed in the gust of a passing train. Rosalla looked up and scratched her head, deciding to ask the passing Clapp for directions. The station name read Netheredge and Ryan felt it was the right way to go.

4

The tunnels that bored underground were littered with blue money which was ignored by the people who trampled over it who were feeling decidedly fucked and bemused, arguing with each other about which way to go unable to find an exit and struggling to accept the fact that they might be here for some time. Some who had been travelling here for years were becoming accustomed to the white light and vended food which oozed freely from every alcove and orifice, one such being a man whose age was hidden behind layers of rippling fat. He was happily going nowhere. To his left buzzed a soft drinks machine and to his right a hot dog stand – all a man of his girth could possibly require in such circumstances. He cursed and wafted his foul odours towards any passers by who threatened the food supply which he constantly stuffed into his ever-open mouth. Ryan kept his distance and frowned at the catheter which wound its way from inside the eater's pants and into a storm drain. Unlike upstairs, the underground system had been allowed to retreat into a state of chaos and bad organisation. The local transport company had long since cashed in its shares leaving the transport system to go wild. Previously prided on its ability to keep good time, its trains now ran on dream time; if someone wanted to get somewhere they had to make the effort to drive the carriages themselves, which caused an eternal stream of hassle. But Ryan pressed on, helped by Irene's rich voice which was now crackling over the tannoy. He had nothing to lose and Netheredge was just twelve stops away.

The mechanical escalator ate its way further into the earth towards platforms and abstract freedom, Ryan receiving a small dose of adrenaline along the way from a certified doctor who, having lost his direction one journey home, had set up a thriving practice on the northbound heading escalator, exchanging injections and sound advice for gourmet food and information. The adrenaline picked Ryan up, perhaps a bit too much, encouraging him to talk to a total stranger who sat in a G-string on the moving stair next to him.

'Netheredge, that's where I'm going. Have you heard of it, mate? Do you know how I get there?'

The semi-nude looked into Ryan's face and slowly shook his head, opening his beautiful lips wide open revealing a toothless, tongueless black hole inside.

'Don't worry about it, mate, there's a map around here someplace. Thanks anyway though.'

The toothless nude shrugged in reply and continued to suck on his high nutrient milkshake drink through a helter-skelter straw.

The bottom of the escalator was the scene of much excitement. A passing film crew had stopped to shoot a short documentary, and crowds pushed and shoved each other, desperately vying for a chance of fame and remembrance. The director shouted orders to his camera crew from his elevated chair through a gunmetal cone, vainly trying to create some poetry out of the chaos.

'Darlings! Please,' he shouted, steadying himself in his elevated chair which shuddered with the force of the wannabes fuming and cursing each other. Nails broke and hair flew through the air as the camera crew was consumed by the expectant hordes.

Ryan stood at the foot of the escalator, looking for a way through. He spied a pretty blonde sitting on the bottom stair of the adjacent broken-down escalator, looking lost and forlorn and examining two of her broken nails, as yet unaware of the smear of red lipstick which gave her a sad clown-like smile. Seeing no way through, and humming with life, Ryan made himself known.

'Excuse me, are you okay? You're looking a bit lost if I may say so. Where are you going?'

'Going? I'm going nowhere thanks to this bunch,' she replied, gesturing at the throbbing mass in front of her. 'This was supposed to be my big break into the big time. Limousine transport, hotels with swimming pools. My agent says if this falls through I'm fucked. Never work in this town again, all that kind of stuff.'

'I'm sure it's just a glitch. They'll do a reshoot; these film companies are loaded.'

The blonde sighed. 'Don't you know anything? This was my big chance. I found out about this ages ago, before this lot arrived. My psychic told me I just need a few frames on film and I'll be immortal, far and away, no hassles. I had a really good feeling about it. I was so close. And now look at me.'

She stood up, tears in her mascaraed eyes, holding her broken nails up in front of her face. Ryan noticed the tiny angel tattooed on her shoulder and warmed to her. Producing a handkerchief from his pocket, he leant across the escalators and wiped the smear of lipstick from her face.

'You don't need this shit,' he said. 'You're better than that.'

The woman's eyes lit up at the compliment. 'Where are you going?' she asked, seeing Ryan as a person for the first time.

'Netheredge – I think.'

'You think.' She smiled and wiped her bleary eyes, smudging the black mascara across both making herself look like Dick Turpin in drag. 'Come on, it's this way. I'm Ingrid.'

5

Ingrid grabbed Ryan's hand and whisked him into the crowd pushing away anyone who stood in their path as if she'd done it a million times before. The throngs soon thinned as the tunnels narrowed and wound downwards towards the platforms.

Platform B northbound had been partly reclaimed by the people and by nature. The absence of maintenance had allowed plant roots from the surface to grow down into the tunnels. Leaves rustled along the tracks, and green vines protruded from the ceiling, coiling themselves around the multicoloured electric cables and weary passengers who slept in abundance on the wooden benches.

'How long before the next train, Ingrid?' asked Ryan sleepily.

'Anytime in the next ten minutes or ten hours. It really depends on who's driving.' She opened her kelly bag, removing a small plastic cube and pulled a dangling cord. The cube inflated itself with great speed into an armchair. 'Great, isn't it? I wouldn't leave home without it,' she said proudly.

'And where exactly is your home?' asked Ryan inquisitively, fighting the day which was fast catching up on him.

'That's a bit of a problem. I lost my ID in the crowd back there. My memory's like a Swiss cheese. I forget. Netheredge sounds familiar though. Please, sit down – I can sit on your lap. We're not heavy, the chair will take our weight, no worries.'

Ryan sank into the inflatable seat and gazed at the graffiti artist spraying away in front of him. The tunnels were lined floor to ceiling with brightly coloured works portraying menacing looking characters, like contemporary gods who danced amid a blur of aerosol clouds, peering out of the walls into the eyes of passers by. Ryan frowned at one such figure who blew picture clouds of ganja smoke right down the platform. The artist himself, covered in different coloured aerosols, was working his way down the tunnel, getting a buzz from the danger and from the fact that his images would be seen by millions whilst his identity would always remain a secret. His green and red face turned and grinned at Ryan and Ingrid who now sat comfortably on the latter's lap. The artist liked the image before him and stored it for future reference before disappearing into the darkness.

Ryan stared blankly after him. His brain had taken a break, unable to cope with the paradoxical situation he now found himself in. Thoughts dreamt up by Ingrid and the other sleepers on the platform had invaded his own. His eyelids heavy with fatigue, Ryan wondered for several minutes whether the activity was going on in his own mind or in the minds surrounding him, an unpleasant thought.

'You really don't know anything, do you, my friend?' said an indiscernible voice. It had been a long day but all the same his conscience was rarely so vocal. 'You'll never get out of her bad dream; you must know that by now. If you thought you knew what lost meant talk to her a bit more – this is not nearly as far out as far out gets. Ryan knows it.'

Ryan jumped out of the chair, toppling Ingrid on to the platform. She awoke with a start and cursed him. Ryan, however, was not listening. The last voice had definitely not just been in his mind. With arms spread wide to maintain his balance he stared in all directions. The voices continued giving him a distinct feeling of fear and disorientation.

'You don't even know where you're going. There's just a long dark tunnel. Going both ways.'

Ryan fixed his gaze on a waiting passenger on the adjacent bench, hiding behind his paper to avoid eye contact – a perfect scapegoat for Ryan's problems. The tunnel was like a whispering gallery; the fucker had been messing with his head. That's how he gets off, thought Ryan, a genuine mind fucker like the ones in psychological thrillers. Ingrid, frightened by Ryan's sudden change in mood, tried to hold him back as he staggered towards the passenger still seeking escape within the pages of his daily. Ryan, possessed by his demons, ripped the paper in half and seized the man by his coat-sleeves, pulling him from the bench. The face before him, strangely without fear, was not dissimilar to that of Clapp which reinforced his belief that this man was *the* head fucker.

'What's your problem, mister? I've had a shitty day and don't need any of your games. Where do you get off, huh?'

The passenger, still passive and unimpressed by Ryan's threatening behaviour, replied, 'I am not the one you are looking for.'

'No?' said Ryan.

The man answered again in silence, only shaking his head from side to side, slowly at first then faster.

The voice in Ryan's head said, 'Don't be afraid; he's been here a long time.'

Ryan's anger dissipated instantly and he stood and let the man down, suddenly shocked at finding himself completely out of character. He wanted to say sorry, but the figure standing tall in front of him continued to shake his head with unhealthy speed. Ryan turned towards the tracks and felt overwhelming nausea as the imposing graffiti bore down in front of him. Ingrid, noticing the deathly pallor of his skin, made her way towards him, took his hand gently and led him back to the inflatable armchair, whispering softly in his ear.

'You should be more careful,' she said. 'We're on TV.' She gestured towards a surveillance camera which swung slowly from side to side on the bracket above their heads. 'Everyone will think you're some kind of crazy person. If you want to travel with me, you've got to get your act together. I've got an image to maintain.'

Ryan stared blankly at Ingrid as she produced a hand mirror from her bag and adjusted her peroxide blonde hair, groaning at her smudged lips and mascara.

'Jesus. We've got some real work on our hands if we want to get anywhere, man.'

Ingrid's fuzzy logic did not make Ryan's mind state any easier to live with. Irene was a million miles away by now – just a faint memory of a real world, a pleasing parallel to the twisted insanity of this one, even though from an aesthetic point of view Ingrid, despite the mad edge, was up there. He had no idea how long he would survive, especially when she dragged him from the platform further into the tubular maze and into a highly polished public toilet facility secured by yet another video surveillance system which scanned the area for inevitable trouble makers.

'Ingrid, come on, it's the Ladies – I'm a bloke.'

'Don't hit me with such mindless trivia. You're a mess – and a stranger – look at you. We can't afford to be by ourselves,' retorted Ingrid, checking the blue tiled room and peering under the cubicles for signs of life. She screwed her face up at her own reflection and hurriedly dumped an assortment of non-animal-tested cosmetics by the side of the washbasin, beginning to transform herself from washed-up street walker back into an up-and-coming movie starlet. The process, though only taking a few moments, definitely made her more pleasing to the eye than her previous incarnation, and Ryan beamed his approval.

'Your turn!' said Ingrid excitedly.

'I'm sorry but I don't wear make up.'

'Course you do.' She unsheathed an eyeliner and grabbed Ryan by the shoulders before he could shy away. Forced to remain motionless for fear of losing an eye while Ingrid deftly darkened his eyes, Ryan withheld a shudder while the pencil did its worst.

'Oh yeah, that works. Wow. It's like we really look like we're going somewhere, really.'

'Oh yeah, right. So where are we really going. I'm lost in your world so you'd better make it a good one.' Ryan took a long look in the mirror. 'Your work does emulate the fact that I'm really spaced. Shit, I can hear the train.'

The pair ran weaving between the human traffic back the way they came. The previously deserted platform was now packed with travellers both lost and found but all coalescing in one unhealthy mass, tactically manoeuvring themselves to increase their chances of a place or maybe even a seat on the forthcoming train. Ingrid, who'd confessed to having many similar experiences before, jutted her chin in determination, producing a small device from her bag which she held up expectantly.

'What's that?' asked Ryan curiously.

'I don't know what it's called but it works like a dream on low voltage batteries and always helps me get a place on the train.'

The tube train whistled, heralding its arrival and the throng sharpened its competitive edge. Sliding doors opened and the people on the platform parted like the Red Sea as a horde disembarked. Ryan paid no attention to the device in Ingrid's hand which was now switched on and had begun to buzz. The new arrivals groaned and dispersed among those waiting. It was like a meeting of two similar but totally incompatible species, mused Ryan as a tall gaunt family eased past. The device hummed more viciously.

'Come on,' said Ingrid impatiently.

There were about three or four rows of people between themselves and the train. Ryan did not rate their chances but still tried to struggle through; however, Ingrid, impatient by nature, was more merciless in her approach. The apparatus in her hand was in fact a low voltage device normally used commercially to stun chickens but now adopted to jolt unwary fellow passengers from her path. Ryan found it quite amusing, albeit in a slightly sadistic way, to watch the tiny blue sparks fly from the two electric points through the clothing of those in front who would automatically flinch sharply and stare wildly around themselves to find the source of their mild pain as Ryan and Ingrid, stifling giggles, stole their way past. The awaiting carriage had been lovingly decorated by a graffiti artist whose style, though similar, was far less menacing than that of the one Ryan had seen disappearing down the tunnel.

Ingrid tucked the chicken prod back into her purse and looked around discerningly. 'I love riding on trains,' she whispered in his ear. 'You get to see such a diverse range of life. Some people have been down here for years you know. Their children are totally unexposed to sunlight and healthy living so they take on the most bizarre mutations and characteristics. Look.'

Ingrid rolled her eyes over to a family of five sitting opposite. The tall orange-haired father figure sported a faded T-shirt advertising the benefits of nuclear energy sat passively munching food as his two younger kids probed him with drinking straws and rubbed their own dinner into his which remained motionless like the rest of his body. Only the man's eyes moved from side to side, reading over and over the wording of an advertisement across the carriage. The nuclear man also had a nuclear wife and another daughter, a teenager who sat, as girls of her age sometimes do, looking disgruntled and angry at the world around, blocking out the familiar ambient sounds with a stereo plugged into her oversized ears. The girl, with the name Helinn printed across her green sweater, sat at an angle pointing away from her mother, who, clearly having lost her self-consciousness long before, was jabbering away at her reflection, mixing of curse and incantation, praying for her journey to come to a quick and painless conclusion.

Ryan, who'd been denied the benefits of family life for some time, found the scene difficult to grasp and felt awkward staring even though the entertainment didn't seem to mind. He brushed away a freelance hairstylist tempting him with a manicure and haircut and spoke to Ingrid.

'How long have we been here?'

'Five minutes,' she answered. 'Patience, Ryan, Netheredge is just round the corner. Anyway, what do you reckon?'

'Reckon to what exactly?'

Ingrid answered in a violent whisper. 'Them, of course – they're so weird.'

'Weird?' Ryan thought about the concept, but did not agree with his companion's analysis. In comparison with the previous events of that day the scene before him was a refreshing norm – until the father figure puked over his shoes an unnatural-coloured vomit, produced by a heavy meal of tube food, which sent his two boys reeling with laughter and mock horror. The man's poor wife remained enthralled by the posters as her spouse wiped the excess puke from the corner of his mouth then resumed his blank stare, leaving his shoes to fester as the train sailed into Redsands station.

'Let's move, Ryan, that smell is appalling. That man needs help big time.'

Ingrid offered the sick man a handkerchief and a care nurse's glance before dragging Ryan into the next carriage which was empty save a couple having sex at the far end, groaning and thrusting in time with the rolling train which now eased out of Redsands platform towards the next destination.

'I used to love sex,' stated Ingrid, smiling reminiscently at the copulating before her. 'But since my search for stardom I have never found the time.'

'We've got all the time in the world,' objected Ryan.

'And I get these terrible back pains. It's just impossible,' retorted Ingrid.

Ryan sighed. As far as intercourse was concerned this had been a pretty shit day. He gazed at their transparent reflections across the carriage – his own handsome but slightly troubled and Ingrid's dizzy in thoughts of the future, spinning around in a world of her own. Ryan was tired, the monotony of the ride urging him to go to sleep. The train stopped at Gantry Road, and neither traveller noticed a dishevelled-looking preacher materialise.

'Sinners. Because I know you are. Save yourselves from this pit of hell. Follow the one true light. The light of Gaard. He will show you the way to your true destiny.'

The preacher, holding a serious-looking clipboard under his arm and an expression on his face that said he had been cross for years, continued his gloomy monologue, quoting people of good standing that nobody had ever heard of and anticipating a time which, as he put it, was verging on Judgement Day. The couple at the far end of the carriage had recently finished their own satisfying ride and peered over the seats at the preacher, smiling in a delighted afterglow. The man dismissed their happiness with a wave of his huge hand, turning his attentions to Ingrid and Ryan. The latter groaned in apprehension.

'Sinners. Children of the black night. You should thank your gods for my visitation here tonight. I know what it's like to have no hope, to be going nowhere fast, but there is an answer. Oh yes. Your salvation may be closer than you think.'

'Take your clipboard and fuck right off out of here, my friend. I really don't need any more bullshit right now,' said Ryan.

'Give him a chance. He looks to me to be a man of great experience; this might be the break I've been looking for,' said Ingrid, clutching Ryan's shoulder and looking into his eyes with a crazy longing. Ryan's heart ached. Though he'd only known Ingrid for a short time they'd still been through some scrapes together and he now felt a definite bond between them. But time was a deciding factor and such so-called men of the cloth worked fast, grabbing vulnerable strangers away from the crowds and brainwashing them with merciless psychological warfare. He watched helplessly as Ingrid grew more and more enthralled by the man's words. Growing negativity on his part only increased her resolve that this man was the answer to her crisis. He promised everything she could possibly want – an audience, support, and a new way of life, a more spiritual and fulfilling existence than the one she lived at present. Ryan watched with a shudder as the preacher rubbed his hands together, seeing Ingrid get sucked into his plot. The train pulled to a stop at Greystones station.

'Here. This is our stop, your gateway to a better life, my child,' said the preacher, beckoning through the doorway. By now Ingrid was smiling meekly. She could hardly remember Ryan being there but looked round to wave goodbye. A tear came to Ryan's eye as he noticed the light disappear from hers, and he was left by himself in the carriage to contemplate his solitude, fighting off a wave of depression which enticed him to wonder what he was doing there in the first place.

6

Netheredge, an attractive station, swept into view and Ryan's heart embraced the open air with an unfamiliar longing. Night had fallen now, and fairy tale lanterns swung around, catching the images on the mosaic tiling. As if time had been stopped for the last few hours, Ryan marvelled at the fact that Rosalla and Irene were still standing on the northbound platform looking confused and asking for directions. He put his previous adventures down to a bad dream and called out through the open window of his carriage to summon their attention. His voice did not carry and was obliterated by the rush of air, the carriage jolted, and he fell back into his seat. Though the train was already halfway into the station for some reason the train was refusing to slow down which teased Ryan's patience considerably. His impatience tuned to rage as his worst fears were realised and the train did not stop. He howled in frustration as his rogue transportation left Netheredge far behind and shot back into another lightless tunnel. Ryan felt it was the time for action, or else he would be beaten by the bullshit and would resign himself to a future in tunnels. Ripping a seat from its frame, he began swinging it around his head into the glass screens around him, which shattered but stayed put. Kicking and swearing like a child refused its own way, he scored the sides of the carriage, cutting ragged grooves into the advertisements and the graffiti. Seeing nobody was in the immediate vicinity, his anger was able to run its course. When his rage finally subsided, Ryan slumped on to a seat and looked wildly around desperate for a way out. His anger turned to dismay as he noticed the rail map above his head which informed him that Netheredge was the final stop on this particular line.

'Shit.'

The emergency lever hung ominously by the sliding doors. It was the only way. Ryan bit his lip and looked around guiltily before rushing over to the lever, pulling it down and ignoring the warning sign. The emergency brakes were activated, producing an overwhelmingly unpleasant screeching sound. Ryan watched the white sparks light up the tunnel, then smacked into a hand rail as the carriage finally ground to a halt.

The sliding doors remained closed but Ryan rubbing the new bruise developing above his left eye slyly opened the door which divided the carriages, and climbed down on to the tracks carefully avoiding the live rail. He heard the fuming driver shout down the train to discover the culprit, but Ryan was made invisible by the shadows as he made his way back up towards Netheredge station. Whilst thinking about the surprised expression he would inevitably find on Irene's face, he could hear her lyrical accent mixed with Rosalla's whisper down the tracks – or maybe it was just the wind or was it just in his head. Ryan paid this reasoning no mind, realising that his senses were being intensified by the darkness.